Our Incognito Queen

THE MEN OF PSYSPECOPS
BOOK 4

KAMERON CLAIRE

SNUGGLE WHORE PRESS, LLC

PSYSPECOPS

OUR
INCOGNITO
Queen
KAMERON CLAIRE
USA TODAY BESTSELLING AUTHOR

Dedication

To all the Witty, Wicked & Wild Readers...
Never let them silence our Witty Tongues,
Never let them shame our Wicked Needs,
Never let them stop our Wild Deeds.
If it harm none, do what thy will!

Anonymous Encounter Kink

BDSM terminology is vast, varied and often up to interpretation. For the purpose of this book, these definitions apply to our submissive and her Dominants...

What is Anonymous Sex -or- Sexual Anonymity?

Some people are attracted to the rush of anonymous sex and feel they lose their inhibitions in this type of encounter. They find freedom in sexual engagements without encumbrance, allowing themselves to experience pleasures they otherwise would not allow themselves. They may also enjoy the feeling of being a sexual object and/or using others as sexual objects without fear of judgment.

ENTES TUERE
PUNIRE IMPIOS

Chapter One

CARLISLE

THE ELEVATOR DOOR CHIMES, and my pulse speeds up as Mike the postman walks in with today's mail. On top of the pile in his hand are three heavy, elegant, and expensive envelopes I know all too well—arriving today as planned.

"Hey Mike." I smile, trying to appear as casual as possible, even though my heart is racing like a jackrabbit.

"Hey Carlisle. How's my favorite executive assistant today?" He leans his hip against my desk and places the office mail in my inbox without a second thought. If he only knew what was in the envelopes, he might not be so casual or look at me with innocent eyes.

"I'm doing good. How about you? How's the weather today?"

He shrugs. "Not too hot, not too cold. The perfect day to walk the neighborhood."

"That's good." I duck my head and glance behind Mike at my two bosses, who sit in their individual offices not twenty feet from my desk. They have glass walls that can be darkened with the touch of a button, but when they're not on a teleconference or in another meeting, they have their doors wide open.

All day long, I sneak peeks of them while secret fantasies involving one or both of them dance through my mind.

With my desk outside their doors, I'm always within earshot, ready to respond to their every need, fulfill their every want. While it's my job, it's also my pleasure because I love them more than I should.

Not that I will ever tell them that.

I've noticed they focus their attention on my desk whenever Mike drops by with the mail. I guess it's an after-effect of all their years of *spy* training. They are constantly on alert and aware of everyone who comes in and out of our office. Honestly, I'm not exactly sure what they did in the military—something to do with security and psychological operations, or PsySpecOps—as I've heard them call it. I guess that's why they are the best in the business, handling discreet client problems quickly and efficiently.

I've been here six months and in love with my bosses since week one.

All three of my bosses.

For six months.

Three bosses times six months equals eighteen months of longing.

Triple the pleasure?

It's more like triple the agony while I pine for something I can never have.

At least, not the way I want it.

"When are you going to let me take you out?"

"What?" My head snaps up, my eyes searching Mike's face for a smirk or sarcastic tilt to his lips, because he has to be joking.

"Dinner. You and me," he motions between us, a sweet and sincere smile on his admittedly handsome face. He's been a flirt since the day I got hired, but I didn't think we were approaching date territory, and I'm at a loss as to how to let him down easy. If I wasn't harboring a huge crush on three totally unattainable men who have rarely given me a second glance, I might be interested.

Unfortunately for Mike...

"I'm not sure what to say."

His smile falls, and he raps his knuckles on my desk. "That sounds like a no."

"I'm flattered, but I'm seeing someone, and I'm not the kind of woman who dates two men at the same time."

Three men, yes, but that's a different conversation. Well, three specific men, definitely—two of whom are staring at me and Mike right now. Then I hear, rather than see, Garrett push away from his desk, his footsteps heavier than normal.

Mike and I turn our heads at the same time Xander growls, "Garrett, get in here."

Garrett's lips are thin and his eyes are narrowed on Mike. With his hands clenched at his sides, he spins on his heel and attempts to slam the door shut behind him.

Only these glass doors don't slam shut, otherwise we'd have broken glass in here at least once a week.

Despite the glass walls, their offices are soundproof, but there's no mistaking Garrett's anger as his arms flail at his sides. Xander remains calm, although his body is rigid in his chair. He stabs his forefinger into his desk, his face tight as he makes his point—whatever that point might be. Whatever he says must get through to Garrett, because his shoulders slump and he drops into the chair.

"What's that about?" Mike turns his gaze back to me, his brow knit into a tight crease.

"I don't know." I shrug, trying to play it off. My bosses are one hundred percent alpha males with different protective sheens polishing their otherwise gruff exteriors. Darian is pure business all the time, and any softness from him is rare and fleeting, but on the rare occasions he's showered me with it, I've melted into a gooey puddle like the wicked witch. Xander is a big, quiet man whose shrewd, assessing gaze makes you want to shrivel up into a tiny ball if he sends it your way, but with me he's also a giant teddy bear—always sweet and thoughtful. Garrett's personable—damn near jovial with our clients—but he also has a short fuse, and an angry Garrett is almost scary, not that I've ever been afraid he'd hurt me. He's definitely the most passionate of the three of them and wears his emotions on his chest.

Xander's door opens with a hiss, the tiny vacuum broken as the seal between the door and glass panel parts.

Garrett stands there, his face blank of expression. "Are we ready for our two o'clock, Car?"

"Yes, Garrett."

"Great." He returns to his office, his eyes barely skimming over me and Mike.

"I guess that's my cue to get back to work." Mike straightens and pulls his mail bag back on his shoulder. "If things don't work out with that guy, my offer stands."

"That's sweet. I'll keep it in mind."

He winks and then walks to the elevator to continue his rounds through this building. I glance to my left, but neither Xander nor Garrett are looking my way, cold indifference radiating from their offices.

FORTY-FIVE MINUTES LATER, I'm greeting our prospective client at the elevator and escorting her into the conference room. Garrett walks in behind us, his slim, muscular body beautifully framed in a tailored gray suit and teal button-down that sets his bright blue eyes aflame. He's got a casual smile and a firm handshake for the client, something that always sets them at ease.

Then Darian walks in looking amazing in his black suit with a light pink dress shirt and monochromatic tie. I love it when he wears pink. The light color pops against his dark skin, giving him a polished sheen. He's carrying his leather portfolio and sets it at the head of the table, claiming his spot and silently declaring his authority.

I move to the client's side, waiting for Darian to finish his introduction.

"Can I get you something to drink?" I ask, knowing that Darian will drink water, Garrett will drink green tea, and Xander will have seltzer water—all of which I already have on the table.

"Coffee with a touch of Baileys?" She gives me a nervous chuckle.

The woman is flustered, and I smile sweetly at her. I'm not sure why she's here, but if they referred her to my bosses for help, it's something that would shred most people's nerves. "I'll see what I can do."

Exiting the conference room, I run into Xander's big, muscled body, his hands instantly wrapping around my hips to steady me. The man is a tank and yet can class it up with the best of them. He's also wearing a black suit, his white button-down collar open to expose his throat. I don't think I've ever had a second thought about a man's collarbone or Adam's apple, and yet I've fantasized about nibbling along every inch of this man's chest and throat for months.

"Is the client here?" He glances over my head, his hands still on my hips.

"Yeah. Darian and Garrett are already inside." I take a small step back, which alerts Xander to where he has his hands. He makes a show of letting me go, much to my disappointment, and flashes me a small smile. He's about to enter the conference room when I grab hold of his bulging bicep. "Is it okay if I knock off a little early today? I have a few errands to run before I leave town tomorrow morning."

He searches my face like he always does and then nods. "Yeah, of course."

"Thanks, Xander. If you need anything, I'm only a phone call away."

"Have a wonderful trip, Carli. We'll see you on Monday."

"Monday." I suppress the nervous giggle threatening to erupt from my lips and turn away, walking as quickly as possible to the break room where we have an embarrassingly well-stocked bar. While I fix the client's coffee with a generous pour of Bailey's, I think about the envelopes sitting on my desk.

I've been planning this for over a month.

Last Saturday, I went to my favorite stationery store downtown, *Papier Fantaisie,* and bought three of the most beautiful invitations I've ever seen. The envelopes are deep red, lined with silver foil and embossed with a delicate black line. I made the invitations out of heavy linen cardstock with crisp clean lines embossed along the edges.

This store is my favorite for many reasons, chiefly their craft area in the back, which allows you to design and assemble the perfect paper memory there in the store. You can also mail said memories from their store, thus providing the illusion that someone who lives on the other side of town crafted and sent these invitations. I spent most of the day creating these three and was sure to use calligraphy to address each envelope. I printed the inside with raised black ink, my words carefully chosen to be direct, but nondescript at the same time.

I expected the envelopes to come today, which is why I planned to take the rest of the week off. If they'd come yesterday, I would have hidden them. Simply put, I can't watch my bosses' faces as they read my invitation to The Access Club.

One, if they see my face, they'll know I am the one who sent them. My bright red cheeks and nervous twitch would be dead giveaways. And two, if they are anything other than excited by the invite, I will die of embarrassment.

It will kill me to be rejected, even if they have no idea who they are rejecting.

Eight months ago, before I had my job here, I went with a friend to a masquerade party at the Access Club.

I had no idea what I was walking into. Frankly, neither did she. The attorney from her office—who she had the hots for—invited us to a guest social night.

At the Access Club, on a normal social night, anyone with an invitation can attend and do anything as simple as drink and dance the night away, or tour the different rooms to sample the different BDSM kinks they have on display. Dungeon masters conduct *tasters* that the public, i.e., non-members, can sample. It's all over-the-clothes style stuff, although I have found people get very creative with the term *dressed* there. There are no full nude demonstrations, no full submission scenes, and no public sex on these nights. Although, when there is a will, there is always a way. There are plenty of rooms to book for whatever the occupants desire and dark corners to play in.

That night, they were hosting a masquerade ball—which is the only reason I went to a place called the Access Club in the first place. The mask gave me a sense of anonymity, security but no real courage. I spent the night watching people, but I never took part. My friend got bound with rope and then suspended from a giant hook in the ceiling—the rope master spinning her until she flew high with endorphins. I was too chickenshit to talk to the man. While people lined up to be cupped, spanked, and caressed with an electric glove, my friend and I hung out in the bar area and watched the men in suits and women in beautiful, slinky dresses mingle.

Even though I had on a mask, I didn't talk to anyone. And I have to say, I was probably the most modestly dressed person there that night. When the attorney found us, my friend ditched me for a corner booth where they made out for hours, leaving me alone at the bar. It wasn't until I gathered my stuff to leave that a statuesque woman named Jenna approached and asked me to work the coat check room.

After that night, I became Ivy, the coat check girl at the monthly Access Club member/guest social. My only requirement is that I wear a mask when I work. It's interesting because I'm not someone who would have the courage to join a sex club, much less take part, but I'm fascinated by the freedom everyone else has while in attendance. I watch people morph into outgoing, confident people as soon as they shed their coats.

I envy them. I really do.

My life changed two months ago while working in

the coat check closet. The hostess handed me three large, heavy garments. I knew them instantly, the smell of Xander's aftershave hitting my nostrils at the same time as I felt the soft, well-worn cashmere of Darian's coat in my fingers. My heart jumped into my throat as I caught Garrett escorted through the heavy velvet drapes into the lounge area.

Are they members? I honestly don't know. I'm not in a position to snoop, and it's not the kind of place you ask those types of questions. I know my heart broke when I thought this was a normal Saturday night for them, but a couple of minutes later, the hostess came back, fanning herself.

"Those guys are hot."

"Are they?" I pretend not to know who she is talking about.

"You're still clutching their coats, so you know exactly who I'm talking about," she grins and bats her lashes.

"Have you seen them here before?" I ask casually as I hang them up and give her the claim ticket.

"No. I think they were invited by the owners, and are not regular members, but I heard they're into sharing women."

"The three of them?" My cheeks flush hot and I bite my lip. Good god. In the last four months I've worked for them, I had no clue they were partners in all things—and I do mean ALL THINGS.

"That's the word. Could you imagine being the woman lucky enough to have them claim, own, and

possess you—inside and out?" She fans herself with the claim ticket. *"You should talk to them."*

My mouth hangs open. "What? Why would I do that? I don't talk to anyone."

"I know," she shrugs. "You snooze, you lose, Ivy. Maybe I'll talk to them since you won't."

That's when Ivy got the bright idea to invite them to a night of pleasure at The Access Club. This is my one shot to live out my fantasy, even if it is from behind a mask.

Ivy is brave enough to invite three men to ravish her for the evening.

Carlisle is not.

Especially when those three men are her bosses.

ENTES TUERE
PUNIRE IMPIOS

Chapter Two

DARIAN

OUR CLIENT, a thirty-year-old woman bullied by her soon-to-be ex-husband, wipes away her tears. My partners and I sit back patiently and wait for her to collect herself. Her story is distressing, but unfortunately, it's not uncommon. An abusive and entitled piece of shit ex who doesn't want to pay child support or alimony uses gaslighting and terror tactics to drive her insane. Even as she tells us her story, she's unsure of what is real and what she imagines.

I exchange a look with my partners, Xander and Garrett, confirming we agree. She's not imagining shit.

The only tricky part of this case is the piece of shit's background. He's an ex-police officer, now a private investigator specializing in insurance fraud. We don't know him personally. Our professional paths have never crossed, but it means he has access to some of the same tricks and tools we'll use to get him to back off.

We run a private security company in the heart of

Manhattan that caters to a wealthy clientele. We're not talking bodyguard work, although if we wanted to hire a handful of guys and train them, we could easily make a fortune offering that service as well. But currently, we have no desire to grow our small firm beyond the three of us.

Well, four of us, including Carlisle—our sweet, supple, innocent, and completely off-limits executive assistant.

People hire us for the things the police have limited resources to deal with. Kidnapping, stalking, missing persons, bullying, blackmail, and the like. Business is good, especially in a city of one point six million.

Our new client is not wealthy. She's not even from Manhattan. She's a schoolteacher out of Queens who won't be able to afford to keep her job if her ex takes the house and displaces her and her children. The only reason she's in our office is because she's the beloved tutor of one of our past clients who will pay her bills to make this right.

After hearing her story, I'm thinking we'll do this one pro bono.

"It was one thing for him to take his frustrations out on me, but the day he hit our daughter Becca—well, that was the day I had to put an end to the abuse. You know?" She sniffles.

"Yes, ma'am." Garrett flashes her a sympathetic smile and pushes the tissue box closer to her.

"I'm sorry. I can't believe I'm blubbering right now. He tells me I'm exaggerating, and that the bad times were never as bad as I remember. He admits to having a temper, but insists he's never been physical with me or our kids. His cop buddies back him and show up in the oddest places, like blocking my cart as I shop in the aisles of the grocery store. One minute they are there, the next they are gone. I come home and things are moved around on the counters, even though he's not supposed to be in the house. I find random medicine bottles in my bathroom and nightstand, prescriptions that aren't mine, and yet my name is on them. There are empty alcohol bottles in the recycling bin, even though I don't drink. What if he is right? What if I'm crazy and imagining things?"

I shake my head. "It doesn't sound like you are to us. Your ex is doing exactly what he has to do to have you declared an unfit mother. If he does that, there is no child support and no alimony. In his mind, you'll lose everything and either crawl back to him and accept his treatment, or have nothing. Men like this can't fathom being challenged, which you did by filing for divorce."

More tears fall down her cheeks. "I had very little family when I got to New York, and he made sure I lost contact with them over the years. He's alienated me from my support network. Even something as innocuous as a mommy play group resulted in a fight. If it wasn't for Mrs. Whittington, I don't know what I would do."

"Mrs. Whittington is a good woman, and now you have us," Garrett says.

Xander and I nod in agreement.

"Do you think you can help me?" Her watery eyes move from me to my two partners.

"Yes. We'll take the information from you today, do some digging, and get back to you early next week with a plan. Meanwhile, do you have somewhere you and your children can stay for a week? Somewhere he can't find you?"

I know that her benefactor, our past client, Mrs. Whittington, has already offered her Manhattan apartment.

"Yes."

"Great. We suggest you stay there to give us time to ensure your safety." I stand and shake our new client's hand before nodding to my partners. "We will take care of this. Your life will be yours again soon."

I say my goodbyes, leaving her with Xander and Garrett. Walking back to my office, I notice Carlisle is not at her desk. I glance at my watch, a bit surprised to find her gone. Although it is past five o'clock, she usually stays until we are done with our meetings. On top of my desk is a stack of mail, a couple of handwritten notes detailing tomorrow morning's meetings, plus three missed calls—one of which is from our old commander Victor Townsend.

The man never gives up.

I bring the notes to my face, inhaling the scent that is uniquely Carlisle. The woman smells like cotton candy or bubble gum, and my mouth waters every time I breathe her in. The day she walked into this office, she infused everything with her fragrance and has invaded my dreams with fantasies of tasting her ever since.

I flip through the mail, half of which are bills, the

other half junk, before I stumble upon a dark red envelope with black and silver trim. It's obviously personal in nature, my name written with practiced calligraphy on the front. I know the postmark—it's from a zip code downtown. Then I flip it over to find a silver wax seal with the initials TAC securing the back flap.

It piques my curiosity as I gently work open the envelope using a pen dagger to crack the wax seal. Inside is an invitation, the front saying nothing more than The Access Club in bold, beautiful calligraphy.

Inside it reads:

You are invited to a night of pleasure at The Access Club

If you accept this invitation, a woman whose only fantasy is to be shared by you and your partners will attend to your every need and desire.

There is only one rule:
Your hostess's identity must remain anonymous.
She will wear a mask at all times, and no questions or guesses about her identity are permitted.
In exchange, she will submit to your every carnal pleasure, obey your every command.

There's no need to RSVP.

Show up Saturday night at nine pm and present this card to the doorman.

Your hostess will take care of the rest.

I sniff the paper, a ridiculous thought running through my head. My shy assistant, whom I've had the dirtiest fantasies about, would never be a member of a sex club; much less invite me to one.

"Did you dismiss Car for the day?" Garrett walks into my office with a scowl on his face.

"No. She was gone when we came out of the meeting."

"She never leaves before we end the day."

Xander walks in behind him. "She had errands to run before she leaves town for her family reunion, so I told her she could go."

"Dammit, Xander, you know I hate not being able to say goodbye to her," Garrett pouts, crossing his arms over his chest.

"You're lucky I don't skin your ass for the shit you pulled earlier," Xander eyes him, his lips pressed into a thin line.

Garrett shifts and stuffs his hands in his pockets, something he does whenever he knows he's wrong but doesn't like being called out on it. "I can't stand it anymore. It's one thing if we can't tell her how we feel and claim her as our own, but it's quite another to sit by and watch another man ask her out."

I shake my head. "What are you talking about?"

Xander rolls his eyes. "Mike the mailman asked Carli out today and Garrett almost thumped his ass for it."

"I can't sit by and watch someone else love her when she should be with us," Garrett grumbles.

"That's not possible." I clench my fist and lean over my desk. "We've talked about this a hundred times. She's not ours for the taking."

"We don't know that," he snips.

I can't talk about this anymore. I know how my partners feel because it's the same way I feel, but the simple fact is, there aren't a lot of women out there that can handle being claimed by three dominant males. And there are certainly not a lot of women out there that three such males can agree on wanting to possess. Besides, she's our employee. One of us coming on to her is a potential lawsuit, but if all three of us spread her out on the conference table and have our way with her like we're desperate to do, we can kiss our business goodbye.

I hold my dark red, highly seductive invitation in the air, waving it in the faces of my two partners. "Have you checked your mail yet?"

They both shake their heads.

"Go check your piles and see if you have an envelope that looks like this."

Thirty seconds later, they're walking into my office with identical invitations in hand.

"What is this?" Xander asks while Garrett rips into

his invitation. I watch his eyes narrow as he reads over the words. He glances up at me and then goes back to his invitation, rereading again and then again, a peculiar smirk spreading from his lips.

Xander looks between me and Garrett while carefully opening his own envelope. He reads it, glances over at Garrett's piece of paper and then looks at mine. "The Access Club? Who is this?"

"That is the question, isn't it? We've only been there twice, both times as guests. I can't imagine who, besides the owners, knows us—much less how to contact us—especially with this kind of invitation."

Garrett's smirk spreads into a full-blown smile. "I know who this is."

"Who?"

"It's Car." He waves the envelope in the air as if it's a trophy. "It's her way of saying she wants us without having to risk some inappropriate, potentially embarrassing office confession."

"Our fantasies have finally warped his reality." Xander frowns and plops in my guest chair.

"Look." Garrett paces an eight-foot section of carpet, something he does when he's excited about an idea he's positive is a winner. It usually means trouble for the rest of us. "There's something I have to tell you, and you're not going to like it."

I sit in my chair and exchange a quick glance with Xander. I've known these men for over fourteen years. We went through PsySpecOps training together and then served our country for eight years as a unit.

PsySpecOps members differ from regular Army service members. Hell, we're different from other special forces units. Our training continues after PsyOps qualification, and includes phases from the Special Forces Q-course. Definitely not for the weak, although honestly, none of it is. They recruit only the best into the small, specialty career field. We were tested and then grouped into teams of three, damn near guaranteed to accentuate each other's strengths and eliminate each other's weaknesses.

We've been thick as thieves since the day we met and rumor has it that men like us—ex-PsySpecOps teams—prefer to share one woman versus date independently. They say it is an unexpected side effect of our training, but it works well for us. As it was, it only took bemoaning a couple of halfhearted dates early on to realize we share eerily similar tastes in women, indistinguishable desires in bed, and identical needs for our hearts.

The first time we shared a woman was while on R&R overseas, and we instantly knew our future happiness required meeting the perfect woman who would want us as we wanted her.

I turn my gaze to Garrett. Of the three of us, he is the most impulsive. "What did you do?"

"Remember the last time we were at The Access Club? It was about nine weeks ago."

"Yeah?"

"When we walked in, there was a woman in a mask working in the coat check closet. She was wearing a modest bustier with skin-tight shorts and although she had her face covered, I knew it was our Car immediately."

Xander is on his feet, his fist clenched at his side. "Carli works at a sex club and you didn't tell us?"

Garrett puts his hands up in a defensive pose. "Shut up and let me finish the story before you think about pummeling me."

"Xander," I say his name with an unaffected calm, but the effect on him is as intended. He retakes his seat, but the tension in his jaw speaks to the anger rising in my chest. Our girl works at a sex club? Why? We pay her well, so it can't be for money. And why the fuck would Garrett allow her to continue when we could have stopped it?

"As I was saying. After we were seated, I asked the hostess to show me the bathroom. When I got her alone in the hallway, I asked her about the coat check girl. She said they call her Ivy, and she was new to the club, but mostly kept to herself. I then paid the hostess three hundred bucks to gossip with her and point out us as men who share everything, specifically our women."

I jump to my feet. "Are you out of your fucking mind?"

"What?" Garrett looks genuinely confused. "I presented her with a rumor and let her imagination do with it as it will."

"She could've come to work the next day and given her notice, Garrett. Did you think about that?" Xander's now on his feet and of the three of us, he's the biggest— and mean as a grizzly bear when he's pissed.

"But she didn't." Garrett gets that shit-eating grin on his face again. "Think about what it's been like the last two months. Our sweet Car started wearing makeup and doing her hair. She got new clothes—"

"And started wearing those ridiculously sexy stilettos she can barely walk in." Xander runs his hands down his face, his posture relaxing instantly.

"Right. Instead of running away, she upped her game and started coming out of her shell. She's been flirting with us in her subdued way." Garrett glances down at the invitation in his hand and licks his lips. "This is her way of initiating the next step that none of us has been willing to take."

"What if this isn't her?" I run my fingers over the elegantly inscribed calligraphy. "This could be the hostess you talked to in the hallway."

"No way. That chick was an exhibitionist, and she had no reason to want an anonymous encounter. This is Car, D. This is our chance to make her ours."

Xander groans and pinches the bridge of his nose. "Now her family reunion weekend makes so much more sense."

I glance at him with my brow raised. Admittedly, I have the least amount of contact with Carlisle. I find her to be too great of a temptation and have done my best to distance myself from her. Unlike Garrett and Xander, I don't like having my control relentlessly tested. "What about her family reunion?"

"Every time I asked for details, she got squirrelly. I know she doesn't have any close family, so the reunion was a surprise. Part of me thought she was going away with a boyfriend and didn't want to tell me about him. But if she has no family reunion to go to, and that was a ruse to trick us into thinking she couldn't have sent us an invite to entertain us this weekend, then her story and body language makes more sense."

"Check out this card stock. She loves this fancy stationery shit." Garrett slams his invitation down on my desk. "Don't fight it, D. We deserve this. We deserve her."

I glance at Xander, who nods his head. "She's everything we've ever wanted. If this is her, we have to go."

"If we go do this, it could end badly." My mind whirls with all the unpleasant scenarios. Nothing about Carlisle speaks to a wealth of experience. One of us would be a lot for her—but three of us?

She might think this is what she wants and, while I know we would take the best care of her and would do nothing to hurt her, that doesn't make our presence any less overwhelming.

"If we don't do this, she'll never forgive us for standing her up."

Well, shit. Xander has a point.

ENTES TUERE
PUNIRE IMPIOS

Chapter Three

CARLISLE / IVY

I GLANCE AT THE CLOCK, my nerves absolutely fried. They should be here any minute, and I can't tell if I'm more nervous about them walking through the door, or them not coming at all.

If they don't accept my invitation and stand me up—I don't think I'll survive.

But that's a problem for later.

I check my mask in the mirror one more time, impressed with the spirit gum holding it in place. It's black and ruby red, which matches my red silk gown. Over the last couple of days I took off from work— supposedly traveling two states away to go to a family reunion that will never happen in my lifetime—I've immersed myself in the world of high-end pampering. First thing I did was cut and dye my hair. Nothing too drastic, because I still have to go back to work next week, but I had them put in highlights and cut layers to give me a more sensual look. Then I had my first wax appointment. And when I say wax, I mean they stripped me clean everywhere. I'm not sure what my men like in the feminine hygiene department, but I figured a blank canvas was a safe bet. Then I got my nails and toes done, something I rarely take the time to do. Last, I bought a couple of good fake tattoos to help conceal my identity, placing them in areas they would never see at work, but also on my wrist and the base of my neck, which they would have noticed in my normal work attire. I'll have to conceal those over the next couple of weeks as the tattoos fade, but it's a small price to pay to have this night.

Three soft, evenly spaced raps hit the door, and I am unsure of how to proceed. Do I sit casually on the sofa and say come in?

Do I open the door?

Should I greet them by kneeling in a submissive pose?

Oh damn, I should have thought this through.

A slightly harder rap hits the door and I snap out of my temporary stupor, rushing forward to open it and stumbling on my ridiculously high heels in the process. I slam against the door, straighten myself, and open it to find Garrett leaning against the doorjamb, a hard expression on his face. His gaze travels over my body, starting at my masked face and working its way down in a slow, seductive embrace. My nipples pebble under his assessment. I'm pretty sure he notices, if the way his features relax is a sign.

He grabs my hand and gently lifts it to his perfect

mouth, placing the most heartfelt kiss against my skin. "You are stunning."

Xander appears behind Garrett, his gaze also drinking me in. His breathing is heavy, moving his massive chest up and down in a mesmerizing dance. "Can we come in?"

I back up and open the door. "Please."

With that one word, I realize a potentially fatal flaw in my otherwise brilliant plan.

My voice.

I forgot about masking my voice, although to be honest, I have no idea how I would do that. These are three of the smartest men I know, and highly skilled at reading a situation, body language, and speech patterns.

I press my lips together, my mind whirling with ideas. Music.

Maybe if I turn on the music, that'll introduce some confusion—a cacophony of sounds to overwhelm that one sense. Slowly, so as not to trip on my stilettos again, I walk to the bar where there is a stereo and turn it on, unprepared for the volume at which it was last set.

I jump and scramble to turn it down to an appropriate level.

Glancing between my two men who make the otherwise large suite seem small, I purse my lips and then risk speaking out loud. "Is Darian coming?"

"He'll be here in a minute. He had some business to attend to."

"Oh." I press my lips together again and glance at the bar. "Can I fix you something?"

Garrett strides toward me, a confident swagger in each step. A small smile plays upon his lips and then he motions to the bottle of Glenlivet on the bar. "On the rocks."

I nod and make his drink exactly as he likes it. I stocked this bar with what I know my men like and spent a whole paycheck on this night, including the room, which was given to me at a significant discount. Not that the money matters to me. This night, this experience, the chance to live out my fantasy with the three men I have no business being in love with is worth more than all the money in the world.

Xander steps forward, his gaze bouncing between me and every corner of the room. I know what he's looking for, because he's done it at every restaurant and building I've ever accompanied him to. He's looking at the security of the room, searching for hidden cameras or anything else inappropriate given the situation, but he's doing it with an air of nonchalance, something he's very good at.

He grabs the bottle of Don Julio and slides it in front of me. "Straight up for me."

I reach for the bottle, but he captures my hand, rotating it so that my wrist is on display. "Interesting tattoo. What does it mean?"

I glance between him and Garrett, who leans casually against the bar, a wry smirk on his lips. On my wrist is a pair of dandelions floating in the air. It was the most popular fake tattoo the studio had, which I felt perfectly accentuated my anonymous persona.

Attempting to mask my voice, I barely move my lips

as I whisper, "People blow on dandelions to make a wish."

He pulls me forward by my arm and lifts my wrist to his mouth, gently blowing across my heated skin. "Can I make a wish?"

I'm on the verge of telling him he can do whatever he wants when there's a single knock, followed by the door opening with an air of authority. I glance up from Xander's mouth to see Darian walk in, closing the door firmly behind him. He flicks the lock before turning his dark brown eyes our way.

"Perfect timing," Garrett says, lifting his glass.

"I see that." Darian's eyes lock onto my wrist wrapped by Xander's fingers.

Xander smirks and places a kiss against my tender flesh before releasing me.

"Can I get you a drink?" I whisper and motion to the bar, my gaze locked on Darian's.

He looks amazing—they all do—in tailored black slacks and a black button-down shirt. He's got the first two buttons undone, his cuffs rolled up to mid-forearm, the veins on his arms bulging as he unclenches his fist and offers me his hand.

"Come here."

I forget all about Xander's drink and give Darian my hand. He pulls me gently toward him from behind the bar and walks backwards until we are standing in the middle of the room. Without a word, he lifts our joined hands above my head and then slowly turns me for their inspection. There's a growl from Xander behind me, a grumbling of softly spoken obscenities that screams approval from Garrett, and a seriousness to the way Darian clenches his jaw. "What should we call you?"

"Ivy." I swallow my excitement.

"Your invitation..." Darian drops my hand and takes several steps back. I'm left standing in the middle of the room, three larger-than-life men watching me, wearing their own masks despite their bare faces. I've always hated how they can easily hide their emotions, thoughts, and feelings from everyone, but especially me.

"Was mysterious," Xander finishes what Darian has yet to say.

"And intriguing," Garrett joins in, pushing himself off the bar to approach me in the middle of the room.

"You obviously know who we are, and yet you want to remain anonymous. Why?" Darian continues.

I bite my lip and clasp my hands in front of my body. Suddenly, I'm very unsure about this plan. How did I think I could keep up a ruse like this to gain a night of passion with these three men who I know will not treat me like some nameless slut they'll never see again? I can't fathom them treating any woman like that, anonymous or otherwise.

"It doesn't matter." Xander takes a step forward, his hand held up toward Darian. "This is her fantasy and if it requires anonymity, then for tonight, we honor her wish."

"And be damn thankful it's us she wants," Garrett adds.

The muscles in Darian's jaw flex, but he nods reluctantly and takes a seat in one of the two wingback chairs in the room. "Fine, we won't ask you your name."

"Or try to guess it," I squeak meagerly.

A faint smile tilts the corners of his delectable mouth. "Or guess. Or ask questions that force you to reveal your identity. However, Ivy," he punctuates my name, letting me know he knows it's bullshit, "we have some rules of our own before we start tonight."

I glance at the ground and nod. "Okay."

"Your invitation said you'd submit your body to us and obey our every command. Is that true?"

I nod again, a faint blush hitting my cheeks while my pussy involuntarily clenches in anticipation.

Xander takes a seat in the other wingback chair, his drink in his hand. "Have you been with three men at the same time before? Do you understand what being with us means?"

"I understand what it means."

"And?"

I bite my lip. "No, I've never been with three men before, but I read books."

Garrett chuckles. "Two men?"

I swallow the lump in my throat. "No."

"Are you a virgin?" Darian asks, his voice hoarse and accusatory as he grits out the words.

"No," I dismiss the accusation with a confidence I do not have. While I'm not a virgin, I might as well be with my lackluster experience to date. I've had sex twice in my life, both times miserable, painful failures that did not require repeat performances. I guess that's what I get for having sex with someone for whom I only had lukewarm feelings.

But I've been in love with these three for six months and my feelings have only deepened over time. While I interviewed with all of them, it was Garrett whom I fell for first. He's a natural flirt and has a way of making a girl feel special when he's talking to her.

It took me two days to fall for Xander, who is a lot broodier than the other two. But the first time he let down his defenses with me and I saw him smile and heard him laugh, I was a goner.

Then there is Darian, who at times I think avoids me. He doesn't task me with work like the other two, doesn't call me into his office several times a day, and never invites me out to lunch—which Xander and Garrett do at least once a week. For the longest time, I thought he didn't like me and only tolerated me because Xander and Garrett praise my work regularly, but then I stayed late one night to help him put a proposal together for a prospective client and caught him checking me out with more than veiled interest. I also watched as the mask of indifference slid into place when his eyes met mine, but later he showered me with praise for a job well done with a hefty bonus on my next paycheck. After that, things were different between us. I stopped taking his restrained approach as dislike and fantasized it was something more.

"I see." Darian clenches his slacks in his fists, his pupils dilated as his gaze roams over me. "If tonight is to happen—"

"If?" I blurt out.

"When," Garrett replies.

Darian looks at his partners before returning his eyes to me. "Before tonight happens, Ivy, we need you to understand what being with the three of us is like. We don't want to take turns with you—although that might happen as well—but the three of us will take you simultaneously. We will stretch you, push you beyond anything you've experienced before, and test every boundary you think you have."

"Every minute will be pure pleasure, sweetheart." Xander narrows his eyes at Darian. "You have nothing to fear from us."

Darian nods in concession. "Every minute will be pure pleasure."

"Do you understand?" Garrett says from the sofa behind me.

I turn my head and then my body, making eye contact with each of them as I do a wobbly circle on these blasted stilettos. "I understand."

"Good," Darian says. "Now strip for us."

ENTES TUERE
PUNIRE IMPIOS

Chapter Four

DARIAN

"WHAT?" she squeaks, her eyes wide.

I raise one eyebrow in her direction, but say nothing.

She blanches and lowers her head, nodding sheepishly. "I mean, yes, Sir."

Dear god. To have those words come off of her lips is the sweetest melody I've ever heard. I glance at Xander, who looks equally affected, and then at Garrett, who looks like he's about to peel off his own skin. Unlike Xander and I, Garrett isn't accustomed to denying himself pleasure, especially when it's in his face like she is now.

We lock eyes, and I smile, tilting my head in her direction. "Do you want Garrett to help you strip?"

She bites her lip. "Yes, please."

Garrett moves in without a sound and is behind her before she realizes he's stood up. He slides his hands up her arms and places his lips gently against her neck. "Let me take care of you, baby."

She moans, her head falling back onto his shoulder as he moves the straps of her gown down her arms, exposing her perfect breasts to us. Her skin is creamy and pale, her nipples perfect little rosebuds, but I'm surprised and more than turned on by the tattooed script along her rib cage under her plump breast.

To my right, I hear Xander suck in his breath and see him clench and unclench his fists against his thighs.

Six months of flirting might have been too much foreplay for my partners, which is why I've kept my distance. I knew she was a temptation too great, even for my legendary control.

Garrett circles her, placing soft kisses against her skin as he moves. When he's in front of her, he gently kisses her lips and then drops to his knees, pulling her gown off her hips to pool at her feet. She's completely naked underneath, which spikes my need to a near breaking point. He presses his face to her waxed bare mound, inhaling so deeply we can hear him.

"Fuck me, baby. You smell delicious. I can't wait to taste you." Garrett glances over his shoulder, most likely aware of Xander's waning control. Garrett might be the most impulsive, but he's never greedy and highly in tune with both of us. "But first I want you to sit in Xander's lap."

Garrett stands up and helps her step out of her gown, her eyelids heavy with a lust-filled haze. He turns and sits her down in Xander's lap. I can tell the moment her brain registers the hard cock pressing against her ass as her eyes open wide.

"That's right, baby. Do you feel how hard you make us?" Garrett kisses her forehead. "Now lean back, so I can taste you."

Xander's arms wrap around her, pulling her back against his chest. He lays his mouth against her neck, kissing and sucking along her shoulders and around her ear while kneading her breasts in his huge hands.

Garrett kneels before them, pushing her legs apart. "Look at how wet you are for us."

He slides his finger along her pussy lips and brings it up to his mouth, tasting her for the first time. My mouth waters as his lips spread into a slow smile. "Fucking heaven."

She rolls her ass against Xander's lap as Garrett purrs his pleasure.

"Oh, fuck," Xander groans as she rubs against his cock. "Make her do that some more, G."

"Spread her wider for me, and I will."

Xander opens his leg, which causes hers to spread and that's all the invitation Garrett needs. He descends on her, his mouth over her clit and within seconds she's writhing in Xander's lap.

I can't merely watch and approach them with my cock painfully hard. Carlisle, or perhaps I should get used to calling her Ivy in my head, has one arm tossed up behind her as she slides her fingers into Xander's hair. Her other hand is gripping the arm of the wing-back chair. Her eyes are closed, and she's panting as if on the edge of release.

"Open your eyes," I say in my commanding tone.

She does, her gaze immediately finding me. I unbuckle my belt and unbutton my slacks, taking my cock in hand. Her eyes grow wide at the sight of me. She nods her head while licking her lips, knowing exactly what I want. Xander helps her lean in my direction while Garrett continues to tongue fuck her beautiful pussy.

She wraps her nimble fingers around me, sliding up and down my length gently—but gentle is rarely what I want.

I wrap my hand around hers and squeeze, showing her exactly how rough I like it. She's a natural submissive, a perfect student, and she pumps me harder before guiding me to her red-stained lips.

"Suck me, Ivy. Ruin that pretty red lipstick by taking my cock deep down your hot, greedy mouth."

She opens her mouth wide for me and takes me as deep as she can. Her eyes water a bit as I bump the back of her throat and I ease the onslaught of my hips, thinking how wonderful it would be to see her mascara-streaked cheeks without the mask. I'd love to watch her eyes water as she kneels before me, choking on my cock as I fuck her perfect face.

Her mouth is pure sin, her cheeks sunken in as she sucks as hard as she can, providing me with delicious friction. She works me with her hand as she pulls her mouth away in a cry of pure ecstasy.

"Oh god," she moans.

"That's right, baby—" Garrett growls between her thighs "—come for me."

"Oh god, oh god, oh god," Ivy thrusts her hips up, her entire body taut in Xander's lap.

"You mean, oh Garrett," he slows down, his eyes coming up to pin her with a command.

She's panting, a bit dazed and certainly confused as she forgets all about my cock and stares back at the man torturing her between her legs.

Xander chuckles as he rolls and tugs her nipples between his thumbs and forefingers. "You better say his name, sweetheart, or he's not going to let you come."

"You want to come, don't you?" I chuckle, unfastening the buttons on my shirt.

She bobs her head up and down in desperation. "Yes, please."

Then she looks Garrett in the eye. "Please, Garrett, make me come."

"Good girl," he smiles and leans forward to grab a fistful of her hair, pulling her lips to his and kissing with her juices covering his mouth. She moans against his lips and my cock jumps at the thought of being inside of her.

Pulling her head back from his with her hair still wound tightly around his fingers, Garrett gives Xander a non-verbal cue before he lets go.

Xander pulls her back against him and shifts his hips so that she slides down his body, her hips tilted and pussy offered for consumption.

Garrett pushes two fingers inside of her and groans, "Fuck me, you're so tight." Then his mouth is on her again and within seconds she's writhing in Xander's lap, only this time chanting the words that will grant her the first of many orgasms.

"Oh, Garrett. Oh, Garrett. Oh!" Ivy arches her back and throws her head into Xander's chest. He seals his mouth over hers, swallowing her screams of ecstasy. She rides out her climax, thrusting her hips against Garrett's mouth, grinding her ass against Xander's cock—and I'm on the verge of losing control.

ENTES TUERE
PUNIRE IMPIOS

Chapter Five

CARLISLE / IVY

I'VE NEVER COME SO hard in my life.

Nothing I've read or listened to, no porn I've ever seen, has gotten me half as worked up as being watched, touched, or desired by these three men.

I want more.

Garrett pulls me onto his lap on the floor and wraps his arms around my back, his hands in my hair, fusing his mouth to mine. He takes my breath away as I taste myself all over his lips.

It's the hottest thing I've ever done.

"Pure fucking heaven," Garrett whispers in my ear.

"Undress him, Ivy," Darian says from behind us. I glance up and notice he has his shirt off, his pants undone, and he's kicking off his shoes.

Xander has also stood up and is undressing.

My gaze slides over to Garrett, and he nods, a devilish smirk playing upon his lips. I unbutton his shirt and push it off his shoulders, laying kisses over his muscular chest. He has a small tattoo over his heart, four interlocking hearts that double as a four-leaf clover. Three of the hearts/leaves are blank, but the fourth sits upright and looks most like a valentine's day heart. It's outlined in red and filled in with an ombré that fades to a light pink. I'm about to ask him the significance of the design when a powerful arm wraps around my waist and hoists me against a wall of solid muscle.

Xander flips me to face him, and I instinctively wrap my legs around his naked body. He claims my lips in a punishing kiss and walks to the bedroom with me clinging to his massive form. Sitting on the edge of the bed, he presses his hard cock against my sticky, wet pussy as he slides his hands into my hair. He makes a fist, pulling almost painfully, and stares at me as if he's trying to see through the mask. "Are you sure this is what you want? Three men claiming, owning, and fucking every hole in your body, virgin or otherwise?"

I stare into his lust-filled hazel eyes, mesmerized by the specks of green that seem brighter than usual. I'm not sure how he does it, but his cock jumps to slap my pussy —a smack to wake me up and remind me he's waiting for my answer.

I moan. "Yes, Sir."

"Be sure, sweetheart, because while we'll make sure you enjoy it, we aren't the gentlest of men and can be a bit much."

I bite my lip, thinking about the multiple times in the office when they were definitely a lot to handle. I'd love to laugh and bring up any of those times, picking on my man like I do when I'm in their office as their executive assistant. Instead, I bring my hands up to cup his face. "You won't hurt me."

"No, baby, we won't," Garrett says from beside us. He's completely naked. His cock jutting toward me as if it were a homing beacon and I'm shelter.

Xander's hand relaxes in my hair and he pulls my face forward, once again claiming my lips. He kisses me breathlessly, dragging his rough fingertips down my spine to cup my ass, spreading and pulling me tighter against him. He rocks his hips, his delicious length sliding between my folds and bumping against my clit. I look down, watching as he rocks himself against me, the head of his cock poking out between us, wet and shiny with my arousal.

"Are you ready to ride his cock, baby?" Garrett grabs my face and turns me to him, claiming my lips with a restrained gentleness that I'll forevermore attribute to him. I don't know why, but a wave of shyness washes over me, a hot blush hitting my cheeks. I look into his expectant eyes, vibrant blue and mesmerizing like the man himself.

I glance down again, my eyes skimming the wall of tattooed muscle on Xander's chest, waiting for the head of his cock to poke through as he slides perfectly against my clit. I nod, feeling the pressure of having three men's attention focused solely on me and joke, "I had no idea you were so heavily tattooed."

"Why would you?" Darian says at my back. "You don't know us, so why would you know anything about us?" The tone of his voice is hard, angry even, and I glance over my shoulder at him with wide eyes.

"Right. Of course, you're right."

"It doesn't matter, Darian," Garrett growls, clearly annoyed.

Darian's jaw is set as his gaze swings to my left. "Of course it matters. This is her last chance to change her mind about what tonight means to her and to us."

He turns his gaze back to me, his eyes narrowing as he stares at my mask. "Right *what*, Ivy?"

Swinging my head forward, I glance at Xander's raised eyebrow before quickly lowering my chin to my chest. "Right, Sir."

Xander's fingers dig insistently into my ass cheeks with my words, as if the spoken submission means as much to him as it does to Darian. Garrett slides his hand under my chin, lifting my head to face him.

I keep my eyes down, shocked that I almost let my identity slip.

Would they put a stop to this if they knew who I was?

Do they already know?

I'm not sure if my anonymity is a positive or a nega-tive at this point. Darian seems to mind not knowing who I am, or my refusal to admit who I am, but Garrett and Xander are happy being oblivious.

Is that a good or a bad thing?

I just don't know.

Garrett slides his thumb over my bottom lip. "You are so beautiful. Now open that pretty mouth for me."

I smile, remembering why I'm here. It doesn't

matter if they know who I am or not, because tonight is for me. I want these men so badly—it's debilitating. Every Monday I'm excited about going to work because I'll be with them again. Every Friday, I'm depressed because the week is over and we have to go our separate ways.

Every morning, I hold my breath until I see their faces, my body wound tight as I wait for the elevator doors to open, hoping—nay, praying—they are there. Every afternoon, I watch the clock as the minute hand approaches the hour, knowing at five o'clock I'll be heading home alone with thoughts of them swimming around in my brain, the smell of them invading my senses and bringing up fantasies that morph into wet dreams, leaving me wanting every morning.

And so the cycle continues, every day, every week, for the last six months.

Licking my lips, I open my mouth slightly, waiting as Garrett pushes one knee down on the mattress and lines his cock up with my lips.

Xander lifts me slightly as he lines up his cock with my opening, prodding me, wordlessly asking for entry. My thighs tighten, holding my body in place, as he rims my pussy with the head of his cock.

He slides in a fraction, maybe an inch, and digs his fingers into my hips. "Fuck, you're going to be a tight fit." Then he throws his hips up, slamming home, stretching me impossibly full with one forward thrust.

I gasp, and Garrett uses my shock to slide his cock past my lips.

Both of my men fill me at the same time and hold still, waiting for me to adjust to my new glorious reality.

I signal my pleasure by moaning and flattening my tongue against Garrett's shaft, pulling my head back to suck him hard while hollowing my cheeks.

Garrett growls and slides his finger through my hair, cupping the back of my head. "That's my girl. Suck me good."

Xander moves underneath me, gliding me up and down his length gently, coating himself in my juices.

Darian stands behind me, his hands cupping my breasts, rolling my nipples between his thumb and finger.

My senses overload as I give my body over to them. Garrett keeps my head moving, and I do my best to please him by hollowing my cheeks and taking him deep. I breathe through my nose as he hits the back of my throat, my eyes watering with every pump of his hips.

Xander places his thumb over my clit and I take over, finding my rhythm and rocking my hips faster as my orgasm builds. "Ah fuck, sweetheart. Your pussy feels amazing."

Garrett fists my hair and fucks my mouth. At the same time, I cup his balls, which tighten in my hand as his cock thickens between my lips. "Fuck, I'm going to come and I want you to swallow every drop. You understand me, baby?"

I nod as hot cum hits the back of my throat.

Garrett throws his head back and roars, his grip on my hair tightening and then loosening as he fills my mouth. I gulp down his seed greedily, pleasure coursing through my body as my pussy clenches, my climax only a few thrusts of Xander's hips away. He pulls out of my mouth, a thin trail of cum and saliva dripping down my chin. He uses his thumb and swipes it, bringing it back to my mouth. "I said every drop, baby."

I lick his thumb and bring my eyes up to his. He grins and grabs my face, claiming my lips again. He murmurs against my mouth, "You are pure fucking heaven, inside and out."

Xander takes over underneath me, his hips coming up harder and faster on each upward thrust. I throw my head back into Darian's chest as my climax crashes over me.

Darian's impassivity melts away as a small smile plays upon his lips. He runs one of his hands up my neck, his finger wrapped softly around my throat, keeping my head tilted up to him. "That's right, Ivy. Come for us."

My cunt clamps down on Xander's cock, and my legs shake. A cry rips from my lips and I pant for breath, locking eyes with Darian, who finally seems anything other than angry and in control.

Xander wraps his big hands around my hips, joining me as he releases deep inside of me. I'm suspended in the moment, one man holding me gently yet possessively against him, staring almost lovingly into my eyes, while the other fucks me wildly, my pussy gushing, soaking him with my release.

I'm pulled out of Darian's embrace to lie flat against Xander's chest. His big hands are in my hair and he's claiming my mouth, his tongue sweeping through, leaving nothing untouched.

I whimper and my cunt clenches as something cold drips over the crack of my ass. And then there is the slightest pressure as Darian circles his thumb over my asshole.

Xander slides his hands down my back until he is gripping my ass, pulling the cheeks apart with each flex of his fingers. He continues to kiss me, distracting me until Darian applies a little more pressure, prodding against the tight ring of muscle. Finally, he slips his thumb inside and I jerk, my body strung tight.

"Relax, sweetheart. We'll take care of you," Xander growls against my lips.

Darian uses his other hand and slides it up my spine as he pops his thumb in and out of my virgin hole. "Do you trust me?"

I glance over my shoulder and meet his eyes. He might be cold compared to Xander and Garrett, but there is genuine warmth reflected in his eyes.

Nodding my head, I press my lips together. "Yes, Sir."

ENTES TUERE
PUNIRE IMPIOS

Chapter Six

CARLISLE / IVY

"KISS ME," Xander whispers in my ear, his breath hot and heavy against my neck. I turn back to focus on him as his cock slips from my soaked pussy.

I mean, honestly, I had no idea I could get so wet.

Our kiss starts off gentle and quickly grows fevered, the intrusion on my asshole morphing from foreign to pleasurable. Without thinking, I arch my back, offering myself to Darian, who growls his approval. He changes to a finger, sliding deeper with every stroke. And then he's using two fingers—the generous amount of lube making everything slick—sliding in and out of me lazily. There's nothing rushed or painful about his care of my body as he works to prime and stretch me for his cock.

Then, to my surprise, he plunges his cock into my pussy, thrusting against me fast and hard as he keeps his fingers steady in my ass. The feel of him stretching me in both orifices causes me to gasp and moan interchangeably in Xander's mouth.

Xander growls and bites the top of my breast when I toss my head back to cry out, and I know he's left his imprint. I wonder if they'll cover me in their marks by the end of the night? Physical signs that they've owned me, claimed and fucked me—giving me a reason to stand naked in front of a mirror and stare at my marred flesh for weeks to come.

I know they've already imprinted on my heart, but the idea of wearing their marks physically gives me a small thrill, too. The idea they will someday fade crosses my mind, making me mourn something before I've lost it, but then Darian slips out of me, the head of his fat cock pressing against my ass, and I'm brought back to the here and now.

His palm is once again sliding up my spine and pressing me flat against Xander's chest. He pushes the head in as Xander spreads me wide with his fingers. Sweat breaks out over my body as I gasp, my eyes wide, body rigid. It's the oddest sensation I've ever felt—a cross of pleasure and pain—well, not exactly pain, but discomfort. Part of me wants to expel him, push him away, and rid myself of the foreign intrusion. The other part wants to push back and bring myself to the pleasure I know is out of reach.

Darian groans behind me, sucking in his breath to say, "Relax. This is going to feel amazing."

I take a deep breath and drop my face into Xander's neck, willing my body to loosen and accept what I so desperately want and have fantasized about for months. The more I coax my body to relax, the further Darian pushes in, satiating a burning need deep inside of me. Once he's fully seated, he pumps his hips a little, dragging himself in and out a fraction of an inch at a time. It's the perfect amount of friction, enough for me to feel overly full and yet not so much to make me cry no more.

"Give her to me." I don't have time to register what he's said before Xander's lifting me into Darian's arms. I'm impaled on his cock, standing on my tiptoes with his arm wrapped around my waist, his mouth on my neck.

Xander latches onto my breast, sucking my nipple in between his teeth.

Garrett sits next to him, his cock hard and ready, pointing to me like a directional sign. He smiles, brushes my hair from my cheek and then leans forward, taking my other nipple into his mouth. His hand travels down my belly and slides between my folds, finding my clit easily, like two magnets coming together.

I'm so worked up, so sensitive, that I jerk in his hand as soon as he touches me, causing Darian to growl in my ear. "Straddle Garrett's cock, Ivy."

My men lift me like a doll and place my knees on the bed. Garrett lies back while he continues to circle my clit with his thumb and flashes me a sensual smirk that promises all kinds of wicked fun, sending my pussy pulsating in rhythm with my heart. "Does it feel good, baby?"

I moan, my eyes fluttering shut as Darian resumes gliding himself in and out of me at an unhurried pace. "It feels good, but has me on edge, like I can't decide if I want to explode or not. I'm overwhelmed with feelings I can't describe."

"And that's good?"

I see the concern on his face, which makes my heart swell. "It's amazing. You all feel incredible."

He kisses me with that restraint of his, a warring combination of love and possessiveness on his lips. "It's about to get a lot better."

He reaches between our bodies and positions his cock at my entrance. Darian slides deep inside of me, filling me, and grips my hips to hold me in place.

With one smooth thrust of his hips, Garrett fills my cunt with his thick cock and I'm stretched wide by the two of them. No one moves as I adjust, my inner walls trembling and on the verge of crashing down.

"Oh my god," I gasp, my eyes wide as I stare down at Garrett.

He hisses, "Fuck, you're tight."

Darian digs his fingers into my ass cheeks and then lands his palm down with a smack, the loud sound reverberating off the walls. He pulls out and then glides back in slowly and all three of us groan out loud. "Talk to us, Ivy. Tell us how you feel."

I glance over my shoulder and lock eyes with him. His dark brown orbs glow with a fire I've only seen occasionally, and maybe I'm projecting my own feelings on him, but they radiate love and affection too. "I feel like I've never been more eager to be split in two in my life."

He smiles and leans forward, placing a series of kisses along my spine. "Sounds like you're ready."

Garrett slides his fingers into my hair and swings my face back to him, kissing me deeply as both men take turns pulling in and out of me. I'm constantly full, overly stimulated, and gushing wet against their impressive cocks.

He pulls my hair, bringing my head back so he can kiss my neck.

The mattress presses down beside us as Xander kneels next to me, our positions a mirror image of earlier.

Garrett murmurs in my ear. "Show Xander how amazing your mouth is, baby."

I lift my eyes and lick my lips, placing a wicked smile on my face. "Yes, Sir."

Xander growls and cups the back of my head, guiding me forward. I take him in my mouth with an eager pull, sucking his cock deep. He cleaned up, leaving only a hint of my scent on his skin, and I moan my desire to make him come again.

I want nothing more right now than to make my men happy, giving them all the satisfaction I can provide with my body and my submission. I'd do anything for them in this moment, my next orgasm building as Darian, Garrett, and Xander quicken their paces, thrusting in and out of my mouth, ass, and pussy with more insistence, more desire, more need.

"Not yet, girl," Garrett squeezes my waist as my cunt clamps down on him.

Darian smacks my ass again, hard. "Don't come until we say so, Ivy."

I look up at Xander with pleading eyes. I don't know

how to hold off an orgasm. Hell, I can barely give myself one when I want to, but stopping the onslaught about to overrun my body?

Not likely.

I try clenching my core, which has the opposite effect. I squeeze Darian and Garrett at the same time, causing both men to growl. Garrett fucks me from underneath, his hips coming up hard and relentless as he pushes me over the edge. Xander clenches his fist in my hair, fucking my mouth around my cries of ecstasy as my entire body shakes with my release. Darian groans, shooting a load of hot cum into my ass at the same time as Garrett stills, his body rigid as he comes, too.

We all hold still, except for Xander, who is chasing his own release between my lips, as wave after wave of pleasure courses through my body. Seconds later, Xander's grunting his own release, shooting cum down my throat. I swallow him down as if on autopilot, my brain too scrambled to make active decisions.

He pulls himself free from my mouth and lets go of my head. I collapse onto Garrett's chest, my bones jelly and my muscles liquid. I've never felt so relaxed and satiated, my only thought being: I hope this night never ends.

ENTES TUERE
PUNIRE IMPIOS

Chapter Seven

"YES, SIR."

Her words reverberate in my skull and a need so primal it hurts grips my soul.

I never thought I'd hear those words from her lips, but to be fair, I never thought I'd get to touch her in this way either. Carli was a fantasy I believed would always be out of reach. And now we're here, playing some stupid anonymous encounter fantasy, which rips away my ability to tell her how I feel.

For *us* to tell her how *we* feel, because I know my partners feel the same way I do.

I'm crazy about her. I have been since the first week she started working for us and I found out she's estranged from her family, who live many states away. We bonded over that little tidbit, considering I don't have any family outside of Garrett and Darian either.

I come hard into Carli's perfect mouth, her body shuddering with the release that my partners have given her. She collapses on Garrett's chest as soon as I pop my cock free from her red-stained lips. I lean down and kiss her head, her cheek, and stroke her hair lovingly.

She's so fucking beautiful it hurts to see her and yet not actually see her. I hate this mask, but not as much as Darian, obviously, because that motherfucker has pissed me off a few times tonight. I understand why it bothers him, but that doesn't mean he has to blow our one chance with her. As much as it will pain me to leave in the morning, I'd rather have this one night than nothing at all.

At least that's what I keep telling myself.

Monday morning should be painfully interesting.

Darian slides out of her and walks to the bathroom. I hear the faucet come on and wait for him to come back into the room. He emerges with a washcloth and gently cleans her before Garrett rolls her to his side. I lie next to her and pull her into my arms, her back nestled against my chest, her head resting on my bicep.

Garrett rolls to face her, and for a brief second our eyes meet. I know Garrett better than I know myself sometimes, and I know he's dying to tell her what we know and that we don't need the mask and now that we've shared what we've shared, there is no going back.

Wrapping my arm tight around her waist, I lean my head forward and press my lips against her neck. "How do you feel?"

She smiles, but keeps her eyes closed. "I feel like I've had an out-of-body experience, and it's rendered me boneless."

Garrett chuckles and slides the back of his hand over

her collarbone and then over her breast. Her nipples pebble into tight little beads instantly, which he pays attention to by sucking them gently into his mouth.

She sighs and slides her fingers into his short hair, holding his head to her breast. I slide my hand down and grip her hip, pulling her ass against me. Instinctively, she wiggles, taking me from zero to half hard in less than a second.

I lift and separate her legs, sliding my cock into the warm junction between her thighs. I push my hips forward and although Darian cleaned her up—a bit of aftercare we're very cognizant of—she's still damp, allowing me to slide between her slick folds. The feel of her wet heat against me and I'm instantly hard again.

She brings her arm back and wraps her fingers in my hair, tilting her face toward me. "Again? So soon?"

I kiss her, smiling against her mouth. "I only get you for one night, so I'm going to take you in every way possible, as often as possible, until the sun comes up."

Garrett growls from between her breasts. "You're going to be very sore by the time we're done with you, baby."

"You didn't think we were one-and-done kind of men, did you?" I raise an eyebrow and smile.

She bites her lip and shakes her head. "No, nothing about you told me you are one-and-done in any way. But I thought men needed more recovery time."

"Some men do, but you were smart enough to pick us —and we have powerful sex drives." I kiss the tip of her nose.

"Insatiable, really," Garrett murmurs against her soft skin.

I chuckle. "Great stamina, too."

Darian walks in from the front room with a glass of water in one hand and a small pink vibrator in his other. "Drink this, Ivy."

She sits up slightly, taking the glass from his fingers. "Thank you, Sir."

I flex my fingers against her hip, digging my fingertips in with that one word, letting her know how much I like it.

Smiling, she lifts the glass to her lips and takes a healthy drink. Then she offers it to me. I take a drink and pass it to Garrett, who is now sitting up on his side, his head propped up in his hand. He continues to touch and tease our girl with his other hand, drawing lazy circles around her breast, keeping her nipples puckered into tight little buds.

Darian holds up the little clit vibrator, his eyebrow raised, a wry tilt to his lips. "Of all the toys and tools available in the next room, which of them did you bring versus which ones were already here?"

"About half?" A blush hits her cheeks, which I find adorable. After everything we've done in the last couple of hours, the fact she is still bashful is sexy as hell.

"Have you used any of them yourself?" Garrett asks, his lips spreading into a wicked smile when she looks at him with wide eyes.

"A couple of them are mine from home—so yes."

Darian turns on the pink one in his hand. It vibrates

hard, the sound undeniable, the setting on high. "Is this one your favorite?"

She bites her lips and tries to suppress her grin. "Sometimes, Sir."

He offers her his hand. I slide out from between her legs and roll onto my back. She takes his hand, and he pulls her to her feet. "Alright, lazy ass. We only have so many hours left in the night and a lot more exploring to do."

Darian exchanges a knowing glance with me and continues. "I want you to go into the next room and pick two toys and one tool."

"Sir?" she squeaks when he lands his large hand on her pert ass cheek with a solid smack.

"Did I stutter?"

"Two toys, sweetheart—one vibrator and one other toy—and then one piece of equipment, like the cross or the bench," I reiterate.

Someone well-stocked this room with many of the toys found on the dungeon floor below. A St Andrew's Cross lies in the corner and a padded bench sits against the back wall. I'm sure there are cuffs, paddles, and floggers on the table near the back, but I didn't take the time to inspect them. I'd be willing to bet good money Darian did and his imagination is running full speed ahead, especially with questions as to what Carli brought from home versus what she brought in to sate her curiosity.

No matter how comfortable we make her, I doubt she'll tell us the truth about her curiosities. At least not tonight, and right now, tomorrow isn't promised to us.

ENTES TUERE
PUNIRE IMPIOS

Chapter Eight

DARIAN

I LEAD Ivy into the living room and to a table with paddles, riding crops, and floggers. There are also cuffs, ropes, and clamps. I can't imagine her being ballsy enough to hand me a flogger, but she might have some interest in a paddle, considering her response every time I've smacked her ass.

She likes it—a lot—and I couldn't be more pleased.

I consider myself a soft dominant, but on the heavy-handed side. I enjoy testing boundaries and accepting submission, but I'll never demand it. Xander also has D/s tendencies, but he's more of a primal dominant, a lot more interested in chasing her, throwing her over his shoulder or pinning her against a wall, but only if it makes her scream his name in pleasure. Not that we've had many submissives over the years. It's hard to find a woman who has the same needs and desires as we do. Garrett is a pure hedonist, seeking and giving pleasure in any form available, but he's been craving the one woman who likes to touch and be touched as much as he does.

She bites her lip as she looks over the selection. Her gaze keeps returning to the large leather paddle with the thin padding on one side, but she's yet to point it out to me.

I place my hand on her flank, massaging in a slow circle with enough friction to warm her skin. With my mouth hovering over her ear, I whisper, "What do you find intriguing? What have you fantasized about before? What scene out on the dungeon floor made you drip with desire?"

She glances up through her eyelashes and presses her lips together.

I grab the paddle. "How about this?"

"Do you want to spank me, Sir?"

"The question is, do you want to be spanked?"

"I think I do."

"Why?"

She drops her chin to her chest. "I'm not sure. I've seen some girls after they've been spanked and they look like they are flying high. Drunk, even. It's intoxicating to watch them."

"Did it make you wet?"

Nodding, she moans as I slide my hand between her legs. She's plenty wet just talking about it. "Not that I plan to take you far, but you need a safe word."

"Cinnamon?" she offers.

I nod, curious why she'd choose that word. "Pick a piece of equipment."

Xander walks up beside us and slides his hand onto the back of her neck. He tilts her face towards him and kisses her gently before pulling back with a smile. "Does this stuff get you hot, sweetheart?"

"I think it does, but I'm also scared."

He shakes his head and runs his finger over her cheekbone. "You have nothing to be afraid of with us. We'll take care of you." Xander exchanges a glance with me. "Always."

I gave him an imperceptible nod, but my stomach sinks with the thought.

Always.

Yes, we will take care of her until the day comes that she's no longer ours. Until the day some man puts a ring on her finger and takes away our ability to care for her. Because that day is going to come and I dread it like I dread death.

Not my death, but the death of those I love.

And the list of people I love is very short. My momma, Xander, Garrett, and Carlisle.

Since we received our beautiful invitations inviting us to live out our ultimate fantasy—well, not our ultimate fantasy, but a taste of what that would be like—I've had a sinking feeling in my gut.

Tomorrow is not going to be a cheerful morning.

This is going to end badly.

I know it, but I don't know how to stop it.

We're here now and, like the greedy, selfish bastards we are, we're going to enjoy every minute and let tomorrow be what it is.

I understand her position. Admitting who she is might be scary, but I don't know how to ease that fear without taking her choice away from her. She's exactly what I want—what we want—and has been from the moment she walked through our door. I've given her multiple opportunities to pull off the mask, but she's unwilling to do it and maybe I need to realize it's not fear holding her back.

Maybe anonymity is the fantasy, and we'd ruin it by telling her we know.

Regardless, I'm not looking forward to tomorrow. And I feel that impending heartbreak is synonymous with the sun rising in the East.

"Maybe we could try that?" She points to the St. Andrew's Cross. Then she points at the bench. "Or that?"

"Do you trust us, girl?" I clench a fist of her hair and lean into her ear, nipping at her earlobe.

She moans, her eyes fluttering shut. "Yes, Sir."

I lead her to a pillow in front of one of the wingback chairs, forgoing the apparatuses. "Kneel."

Xander sits in the chair, and I motion to his legs. "Chest and stomach on his thighs, ass in the air."

She's average height, and not tall enough for her ass to be where I want it, but they stocked this place for practically every need. Garrett sees it before I do and grabs a short ottoman, sliding it beside her. He offers her his hand and brings it to his lips, placing a sweet kiss against it as she stands. He moves the ottoman in place and helps her resume the position. We drape her body over

Xander's lap, her head to the side facing Garrett, who sits in the other chair, while we hold her ass up high and in perfect supplication.

I lean forward and whisper in her ear. "Are you sure you want to play?"

She nods her head against Xander's thigh. He strokes her head and plays with her dark chestnut hair, but brings his eyes to me. I can see the fire in them, his excitement ramping up much like my own.

"What's your word?"

"Cinnamon," she breathes.

I hand Xander the small clit vibrator and he slides his hand down her spine and between her legs. "Spread your legs a little, sweetheart."

"Yes, Sir," she says and does exactly as he requests, and I note the small smile curving his lips. Yeah, he gets off on the shit just as much as I do.

He slides the vibrator against her clit and turns it on, her entire body jerking in surprise. Her hips curve forward as she presses down on the toy and her ass wiggles as she attempts to align it to her clit.

I shake my head and Xander pulls it away.

She whimpers.

"Ass in the air, girl," I say, rubbing my palm against her left cheek to warm her up.

She complies beautifully, and I bring the paddle down against her primed flesh.

Her body jolts from the impact, her ass cheeks clench and she gasps as her head comes up. I follow immediately with another smack, taking advantage of her surprise.

Xander soothes her by holding her flat against his legs with his fingers splayed between her shoulder blades.

Garrett walks over and sits in front of her on the ground, offering her his hands. "Take my hands."

She does and I love it, because it stretches her body out over Xander's lap. It also means he's watching her eyes and counting her breaths, absorbing her pleasure.

He kisses her gently and smiles, but says nothing.

I rub my palm over her reddened flesh, feeling the heat come off her skin. I'm fairly certain she has not been spanked before tonight and I want to ease her into the experience.

I want to ease her into a lot of things, but that's out of my control at the moment, and I hate it.

I pull my hand away and bring the paddle down two more times until she's squirming and whimpering beneath me.

Xander doesn't even have to make eye contact with me to know what comes next as he slips his hand once again between her legs, pressing the small vibrator where she needs it most.

She involuntarily bucks her hips forward, fucking the small vibrator and chasing her release. I rub my hand over her right flank, priming it, and then give Xander a silent nod. As soon as he removes his hand, she sags against his thighs, and I deliver three softer swats in rapid succession.

Ivy cries out, her body strung tight between the three of us. Garrett kisses her knuckles and then leans forward to claim her lips. I can tell by the smile on his face she's glassy eyed, a light sheen of sweat breaking out over her skin. Xander slides his hand into her hair and pulls her head back. She moans and then I deliver another two smacks to her right ass cheek before taking a step back.

Xander keeps his grip on her hair as he slides the vibrator back between her slick folds. Her body glistens with her arousal, and I kneel behind her, massaging and separating her ass cheeks with my hands.

Then I slide two fingers inside of her, stroking her g-spot and sending her over the edge. Her entire body quivers as she cries and whimpers through her climax. She's dripping, her come gushing out over mine and Xander's hands. It causes a growl to rip from my throat, as I want nothing more than to plunge my cock deep inside of her.

But this is her first time in something close to subspace with us and I want to care for her as she comes out of it. With Xander's help, I hoist her into my arms and carry her back into the bedroom. Over my shoulder, I hear Garrett say, "We should ask her to remove the mask and tell us her name. She'd tell us anything right now."

"You know that violates the trust she's given us tonight. Where the fuck's your head at?" Xander growls.

Garrett snaps back. "I know that, but this entire evening is frustrating as fuck. We have her. She's perfect. And then what? We're going to walk away in a few hours?"

"Yes," Xander hisses.

I lay Ivy on the bed and sit down beside her, my back pressed up against the headboard. Her eyes are closed, but she rolls into me, putting her head on my lap and clutching at my body as if I were a giant teddy bear.

A teddy bear, I am not.

This really should be Xander lying here holding her close, or Garrett stroking her hair, waiting for her to come back to me—to us—because this is the memory that will break me come Monday morning.

ENTES TUERE
PUNIRE IMPIOS

Chapter Nine

CARLISLE / IVY

I REGAIN—WELL, not exactly consciousness because I never passed out, but awareness minutes later. Even though I was awake, I wasn't exactly present when my orgasm crashed over me either. It was like having an out-of-body experience—everything and nothing touching me at the same time—and when I came, my body let loose a pent-up orgasm that wrecked my soul.

Laying with my head on Darian's lap, I come to knowing warmth and tenderness under his touch. At my back is Garrett, cocooning me with his body heat, his arm draped over my waist, hand cupping my breast. I open my eyes and see Xander sitting in a chair with his slacks on, watching me as my eyes regain focus. His expression betrays nothing until I smile, and then a softness I've seen a few times in the office takes over his features. A quick shared intimate moment when he lets down his defenses for me—only me.

Sighing, I tilt my head and lock my gaze with Darian's dark brown ones. He smiles and caresses my cheek. "How do you feel?"

"Thirsty."

Xander leans forward and offers me a glass of water. Parched beyond belief, I gulp it down, spilling out of the corners of my mouth.

I dribble on Darian's lap and he jumps, the cold water splashing against his semi-hard erection. "Careful, girl, or I'll make you lick it up."

Emboldened, I lick my lips and hand my empty glass back to Xander. "I can do that."

"You're not tired?" He raises his brow.

Garrett moves behind me, his hand curving over my hip and dipping between my legs.

I can't help it. I push my ass back, finding him hard and ready.

How these men can get and stay hard like they do amazes me. I honestly didn't know it was possible with mortal men. I thought it was only a trick of the porn industry or fantasies out of romance novels.

"Strangely, no. I feel renewed. Reinvigorated."

And unbelievably horny.

Darian's cock hardens and rises to my lips, as if I pushed the magic button. I take him deep, sucking him into my mouth as Garrett's fingers circle my clit. It takes no time to get me worked up, my neurons firing at a thousand percent.

Strong fingers wrap around my hair, pulling me off Darian's cock. "I guess you're not tired."

I'm panting, completely focused on pleasure—giving

and receiving—all the shyness and hesitation from earlier gone. I feel primal, like a caged lioness ready to pounce, and I'm starving for these men. My men. My everything. "I need you. All of you. Now."

Darian and Xander exchange a knowing glance as Garrett rolls me to my back and kisses me. He's moving down my body so fast that I don't even have time to register it before his mouth is on my pussy, sucking my clit hard against his teeth. I cry out, arching my back, my orgasm coming quickly on his lips.

Reaching out, I find Darian on his knees next to my head, waiting. I grab hold of him firmly and wrap my fingers around him tightly, pumping hard as Garrett sits up and wipes my juices from his face.

"Fucking heaven," he says and then crawls back up to lie beside me. He rolls me toward Darian so I'm on my side, and catches something Xander tosses in the air behind me. They move like a precision unit—one mind and singularly focused.

Me.

Then cold, slick fingers slide down my ass crack and circle my asshole. The first digit of Garrett's finger pops in and out of the tight muscle with more surety than before. I pull Darian to my mouth and continue to lick and suck as Garrett primes my ass for his cock.

Everything is moving faster this time, raw and animalistic, as if they are feeding on my need and feeling my desperate desire race through their veins. He lines his cock up and pushes forward, pulling my thighs apart to grant him better access as he pops the head through the tight ring of muscle.

I whimper around Darian's cock and glance up as he gathers my hair in his fist. "Good girl. Keep sucking."

I do, without hesitation.

Inch by inch, Garrett pushes inside me, cursing as he does. "Fuck, you're so goddamn tight," he hisses against my neck, pulling me on top of him once he's deep inside of me.

Darian hovers over us and shoves his cock back in my mouth, using the angle of my tilted head to slide easily down my throat.

Xander comes up between my legs, pushing my thighs farther apart, which causes me to sink down even further onto Garrett's cock, taking him to the hilt. Then he thrusts his cock into my pulsating cunt soaked with my arousal. I come immediately—sticky, silky liquid pouring out of me as both men thrust in and out at a fevered pace. No longer are they gentle as we become one, but instead we take our pleasure from each other as quickly as we can.

Garrett cups my breasts, pinching and teasing my nipples as Xander grips my waist, his fingers digging into my hips. They continue to pump into me through my orgasm, in and out in a maddening rhythm that instantly takes me right back to the edge.

I'm going to come again, I realize.

Twice, maybe three times in a row, something I didn't believe possible—and I'm so greedy for it, I want to scream.

Darian comes first, shooting cum down my throat. I gulp him down quickly, gasping for air when he pops free from my lips. He cups the back of my head and lifts it so my eyes lock onto Xander's cock as he pumps in and out of me. Growling, he lowers his mouth to my ear. "Look at you, Ivy. Look at us. See how fucking hot you are being fucked by us? I wish we had a mirror overhead so you could see what we see. We own you. Every part of you. Inside and out, you are ours—mind, body and spirit."

His words, their meaning and intensity, cause the veins in Xander's neck to bulge as he releases inside of me with a roar. I come again as his cock jerks against my inner walls, my pussy clamping down and pulsing around him, which causes Garrett to come, jerking hard and thrusting his hips underneath me.

It's wild and untamed, barbaric and beautiful as we come together—panting, moaning, and growling through our releases.

Quiet washes over us, even though nothing has changed. Xander and Garrett are still seated fully inside of me, our come mixed and dripping out of every hole. Xander looks over my head at Darian, his raw and open features fading away, his mask sliding back into place. Garrett sighs heavily underneath me, his body going limp, and runs his hands gingerly up and down my chest. Darian lets go of my hair and glides his fingers gently across my lips before sliding off the bed.

Within seconds, the sexually charged chaos dissipates, leaving me chilled despite the sweat on my skin. Xander pulls out of me and stands at the end of the bed.

Garrett rolls me to the side so he can pull out of me too, and suddenly I'm empty and alone.

They pull me into a seated position. Garret wraps his arm around my waist and holds me upright.

Xander leans forward and kisses my head. "Are you okay?"

"Yeah."

"We didn't hurt you?"

I glanced from him to Garrett to the bathroom, where I hear Darian turning on the shower. "No. That was amazing. I've felt nothing like that in my life."

He lets out a deep sigh and pulls me to my feet. "Good. I was worried we had lost control there."

Garrett stands up beside me. "Come on. Let's clean up and then we can snuggle in bed for a while."

They walk me into the steamy bathroom where Darian is already rinsing off under the hot shower. He steps out and Xander steps in, pulling me in behind him. He rinses off quickly, forgoing the soap, but handing it to Garrett, who lathers up his hands. It's Garrett who washes me gently, taking special care as he runs his hands between my legs. "You are going to be very sore later."

I lean back into Xander's chest and sigh as Garrett pulls my leg up. "I'm sore now."

"Epsom salt baths," he says as he rinses me clean. "A lot of Epsom salt baths."

Xander takes the towel Darian offers and steps out of the shower, holding his hand out to me. I take it and step out as he wraps me in the towel. Twenty seconds later, Garrett is turning off the shower, quickly rinsing himself as well. I'm curious why, but I don't ask, the unbridled carnality of the last half hour replaced by tender aftercare.

"Let's relax for a bit." Xander leads me out of the bathroom wearing a towel around his waist. Darian is standing next to the bed, the bedspread pulled off the bed, the sheets turned down.

"Are we going to sleep?"

He shakes his head. "No. Just resting."

I drop my towel and slide into the bed, squirming toward the middle. Xander slides in behind me and pulls my back against his chest.

Garrett slides in on the other side and faces me, tilting his forehead to touch mine. He kisses me gently and smiles, stroking my cheeks under the mask with his fingers. "You are so lovely. Isn't she lovely, Xander?"

"Perfect in so many ways."

Darian sits on the bed behind Garrett, his back propped up against the headboard. He keeps his hands to himself, but looks down at us with an almost paternal eye. My energy is depleted as I come down from the events of the night, my brain too tired to capture every detail and before I know it, my lids are too heavy to keep open and I let them close, wrapped in the warmth and comfort of my men.

ENTES TUERE
PUNIRE IMPIOS

Chapter Ten

CARLISLE / IVY

I DOZE off for twenty minutes, maybe longer, and wake up alone in bed. As far as I can tell, I've been alone for a while. Garrett is no longer lying beside me and stroking my face. Xander is no longer behind me, holding me close.

But I know I'm not alone, because I hear the deep masculine timbre of their voices in the other room.

I sit up and touch my face, surprised my mask is still in place. This spirit gum is extra and I'm hoping it doesn't damage my skin when I take it off.

Part of me—the confident, sexually experimental Ivy—thinks I should take it off, walk into the living area and present myself to my men. After the excellent care they took of me tonight, I can't help but wonder if the fantasy can live on in the daylight.

But the other part of me—the realistic, awkward, and shy Carlisle—can't risk the rejection. What if they aren't happy that the body they've thoroughly pleasured and explored all night belongs to their executive assistant? What if Darian gets angry, or Xander turns away from me, or Garrett feels cheated by my betrayal? Because let's face it, omission is a betrayal. Just like lying, and the only reason I get a free pass is because I predicated this night on the agreement that hiding my identity was non-negotiable.

We agreed to one night of anonymous pleasure—and that is what we got.

Fastening the belt on the terry-cloth robe draped for me at the edge of the bed, I shuffle to the door and stop when I catch a part of the conversation I doubt I'm supposed to hear. I peek through the crack in the doorway to find my men in different states of dress. Darian's completely dressed, his shirt tucked but unbuttoned. Xander is putting on his shoes, his shirt draped over the arm of the sofa. Garrett has his pants on, but nothing else. He's clearly annoyed, standing with his hands on his hips. I can see Garrett's profile, Darian's back and Xander's bicep from my perch, but that's it.

"We should go now while she's asleep," Darian says, his throat tight, words strained.

"Now?" Garrett grumbles. "Can't we stay a little longer?"

Xander shakes his head. "It's daybreak. We've done our job, thoroughly used and pleasured her like the invitation said. Now it's time to go home."

"But—"

Standing up, Xander grabs his shirt and pulls it on. "G, this was her fantasy—one anonymous night with the three of us. She got what she wanted. What comes next is not up to us."

I suck in my breath. Is now the time?

Do I go out there and make my presence known?

"Nothing comes next," Darian says, knocking the wind out of me. "One night. That's what the invitation said, and that's what we agreed to. Once we walk out of this door, this night, this fantasy is over. I don't want to dwell on what we did anymore."

I stumble back into the bedroom, my eyes filling with tears. Garrett might want me, or the idea of me, but Darian and Xander seem pretty content with letting this be a one-time thing. My heart shatters into a million pieces as the fantasy of having more with them crumbles before me. I hear some more grumbling, but I can't make out their words with the blood pounding in my head.

I feel a headache coming on, foresee spending the day in bed, and suddenly want this night to be over.

I need them gone.

Yawning loudly, I purposely stumble into the door, kicking it shut before reopening it. I walk out of the bedroom to find all three men turned toward me, Darian and Xander completely dressed, their unaffected masks firmly in place.

Garrett speaks first. "You're up."

I fix my face with a smile. "Yeah, I can't believe I nodded off like that. So rude of me."

"Well, we wore you out." He smiles, but it doesn't reach his eyes.

Xander swallows audibly and walks toward me with

Garrett's shirt in his hand. He shoves the shirt into Garrett's chest and pulls me into his side with a one-armed hug like half-assed friends give and not lovers who explored every inch of each other. "Hey, sweetheart. We had fun last night, didn't we?"

"We sure did." My voice cracks as I fake a nonchalance I don't feel.

He leans down and kisses my cheek. "Thanks for picking us to fulfill your fantasy."

"Yeah, thanks for coming." I blush at my double entendre, the tension flowing off these three men too palpable to ignore. I need to get them out of here, now, before the waterworks start and I cry myself into hiccups. "So, uh, I have to return the room soon and should probably clean up before I do that."

Darian tilts his head toward the door, but his eyes are on the floor. "We were about to take off. We didn't want to wake you, but since you're up..." He walks over and gives me a one-armed hug like Xander, pulling me to his side and kissing my other cheek.

They both let go of me at the same time, and the coldness I feel from the lack of their touch sends chills up my spine. Opening the door, Darian walks out first without looking back and grunts over his shoulder, "Hurry up, Garrett."

Xander follows behind him, but at least has the decency to look over his shoulder and give me a small smile. The door closes, and I'm alone with Garrett as he slowly pulls on his shirt. His jaw is tight and his eyes burn with anger as he stares at the carpet in front of him.

"Did you have a good time?" I ask, because I have no idea what else to say. I can't stand to see Garrett angry and, even though I'm not sure why he is, I don't like us ending our night together this way.

He looks over at me, his gaze trailing up and down my body, his face relaxing a bit. "It was the best time of my life, baby."

I bite my lip and kick at the carpet with my toe. "I'm sorry it's over."

He takes a deep breath and sits down, pulling on his socks and shoes. "Does it have to be? Over, that is."

"Well, the invitation asked for one night, right? I can't expect you to give me more than you already have."

There's silence between us as he finishes pulling on his shoes. He stands up, faces me, and, although there are only a handful of steps between us, he feels a million miles away. "This is such bullsh—"

Xander steps through the door and clears his throat. "Your ride is waiting, G."

Silent tears fall as I stand still and wait for someone to make a move. Garrett runs his fingers through his hair, his shirt clenched in his fist, and walks out the door without another word or a kiss goodbye.

I stare at the door for an eternity—the tears coming faster as every second ticks by. When they don't come back, I turn on my heel and run into the bathroom, turning on the shower to its hottest setting. Then I grab the spirit gum remover and a handful of cotton balls and work on removing the mask that now represents the best and worst night of my life. The bathroom fills with steam as I work around the edges of the mask, finally pulling it off in a painful rip that takes off the end of my eyebrow. I don't care about my face, though, not when my heart hurts so badly.

Stepping into the shower, I take the soap and shampoo down to the floor with me as I finally let the tears loose; sobs racking my body. I bawl until the shower water cools and my cries have turned to hiccups. Even after I turn the water off, I continue to sit on the tile floor and cry until my head pounds from the effort. When I don't think I have another teardrop left, I stand and pull on my robe before flopping down on the bed.

I wasn't lying about needing to turn the room in, although I have a little more time than I let on. Otherwise, I'd be content to lie down and inhale their scent from the sheets until I feel asleep again.

There's a rap at the door and my heart stills as I hear a key enter the lock.

"Ivy?" I hear Jenna enter the room.

"In here," I call from the bedroom.

"Hey honey, how was your—" Jenna walks through the door and stops. "Son of a bitch. What happened?"

Her partner John is beside her in seconds, his eyes zeroing in on my face. "What the fuck?"

I touch my face, feeling the heat and puffiness of my tears, remembering the red marks left behind from removing the mask. "Oh."

"Did those motherfuckers hurt you?" John takes a step forward, but Jenna puts her hand on his forearm.

"Oh god, no! No, no. No, no, no," I stand quickly, my

head spinning from crying and the resulting headache. "They didn't hurt me. They'd never hurt me."

"Then what's going on, sugar?" Jenna's forehead furrows in concern.

"I'm just..." I shrug.

She gives me a small smile. "Did you have a nice night?"

I nod, a few residual tears filling my eyes. Where the fuck do these things come from? I thought I was wrung dry. "It was the best night of my life and I guess I'm sad it's over."

"Oh, honey," Jenna walks forward and pulls me into her arms. "That's kind of the point of this place—to live out your fantasies, but that doesn't have to mean it's over. Tonight was one fantasy. Next time, it'll be another fantasy. And another and another, until you're too old to have any new fantasies."

John chuckles. "And if you're lucky, you'll never be too old to fantasize about the kinky shit you want to do."

Jenna lets go of me and gives her man an exasperated sigh and shake of her head. "Spoken like a kinky old man."

"You're damn right," John winks and smacks her ass before walking out of the room.

She rubs her hand up and down my arm. "You ready to pack up for the day?"

"Yeah. Let me get dressed and then I'll clean up. I should be out of here within the hour."

"Okay," she presses a kiss on my temple and then releases me. At the door, she stops and looks over her shoulder. "You know, Ivy, I was once inexperienced like you. This lifestyle, it's not for everyone and there's a lot more to it than 'him plus me plus a baby makes three.' The only way you can survive is to have open communication and be completely honest about what you want and what you need. When you told me you wanted to have anonymous sex with three men, my warning bells went off, because you started whatever this is with a lie. You took from them their choice to want and be more the moment you sent them those invitations. You've already dealt the deck, and I'm not sure how you want the game to end, but it's probably not going to go as you'd hoped."

I nod, turning to strip the bed. I know she's right, but it's not something I can process right now. In less than twenty-four hours I'm going to have to walk into that office, look three men who have stolen and broken my heart in the face, and pretend like everything's okay.

Before last night, I thought I could do it. But now that I've lived out my fantasy, exactly as I outlined it, I'm not so sure.

ENTES TUERE
PUNIRE IMPIOS

Chapter Eleven

GARRETT

I JUMP out of my car with a dozen red roses in one hand and a four pack of cinnamon strudel muffins in the other. They're Car's favorite and after going round and round with my partners for hours last night, I have full permission to woo the fuck out of our woman today.

I have it all planned out too, starting with some innocent flirting and gentle teasing until she either comes clean and admits the entire charade from Saturday night, or until I have her ass up, bent over the conference table, sucking on her clit until she begs us to claim her as our own.

Either way, I fully intend on tasting her again before dinner.

I walk across the lobby, wave to the security guards, and ride the elevator up, giving a friendly nod to the blonde who is riding up with me.

"Beautiful roses," she gushes.

"Thanks. They are for someone very special," I say,

deeply inhaling their fragrant bouquet as the elevator stops on the seventh floor and she exits the car.

Less than a minute later, I'm whistling as I ride the car up to the ninth floor. I smile, fully expecting to find Car at her desk, her beautiful pale lips smiling back at me as she does every morning. But I'm disappointed when the doors open and she's not there. That's okay, she's probably prepping the conference room or fixing her coffee in the break room. Peeking into the conference room to find it empty, I swing by the break room—also empty—before I stop at Car's desk.

Something is different, and I take a few seconds to realize what it is.

Everything's gone.

While Carlisle kept her desk clean and professional for our clients, she also kept a row of fancy, unused notebooks on the shelf behind her desk, organized by color and size in her peculiar way—and they're gone. Then I look for her rose gold pen cup filled with a dozen fancy pens, also gone. And her coffee mug—the one Xander and I bought her a few months ago that said *Office Queen* —gone.

I set the roses and the muffins on her desk and storm into Darian's office. Xander is sitting in a chair, and both of my partners look utterly defeated.

"Where is she?" I demand, my hands clenched into fists at my sides.

"Gone," Xander says, his voice hollow.

"What do you mean, gone? Where did she go?"

Darian stares at me, but says nothing.

"We don't know, G. Security logs show she came in yesterday around four pm. She cleaned out her desk and left us this note." Xander motions to a piece of paper on Darian's desk.

I snatch it and read.

Dear Darian, Xander, and Garrett,

Thank you for being the best bosses a girl could ask for. I've truly loved working for you over the last six months and wish you all the best in your business ventures.

There is no easy way to put this, but I'm giving my notice, effective immediately.

Unfortunately, something came up last week, and I'm not in a position to give the standard two weeks I'd prefer to give. But I have posted my position on the job boards and have already vetted a couple of worthy applicants I think you will appreciate. Their resumes are attached, and to ensure my absence causes as little disruption to you as possible, I've scheduled three interviews for you later this week.

Again, I apologize for my unprofessional departure.

I wish I could handle this differently, but I cannot.

Respectfully, Carlisle

I read and reread and then read the words printed in my hand again, but no matter how many times my eyes trace over the black ink, I can't comprehend their meaning.

"What the fuck?" I glance at my partners and then back at the note. "What the actual fuck!"

"Calm down, G," Xander says, but his words hold no heat.

"So, neither of you have talked to her since we left The Access Club?"

"Of course not," Darian finally speaks. "We agreed to wait until today."

"Then—" I hold the paper up in the air and shake it as if I can change the words. It does me no good, my heart shattering into a million pieces. The energy drains out of my body, making me limp and lifeless, like Xander and Darian.

I thought I'd been brokenhearted before, but I was wrong. Leaving Car Sunday morning sucked, and it hurt, but it did not break me. This hurts worse than the bullet I took in Iraq. My heart shreds as the emptiness this notes leaves behind weighs on me.

How can emptiness feel so heavy?

I crumple up the paper and throw it at the wall before sinking into a chair. Then I blow out my breath and drop my chin to my chest, mumbling more to myself than to them. "What the fuck?"

FOR THE NEXT few weeks we throw ourselves into our client's case, gathering the evidence her lawyer needs to not only destroy his claims that she's an unfit mother, but to file criminal charges against him and three of NYPD's finest for stalking, menacing, and harassment.

Douchebags.

I've done everything I can to stay out of the office, volunteering to run down every lead, collect every piece of information, interview every potential witness. The simple fact is, I can't handle walking off of that elevator and seeing her empty desk. Every time I do, it breaks my heart, and I'm filled with a rage so visceral, I shake.

How could she leave us like that, especially after the night we shared? I replay those near perfect hours over and over again in my mind. I thought we treated her mind and body well, taking the best care of her while giving her a taste of everything we have to give.

She seemed to like it.

No fuck that—she seemed to love it.

Sure, the way we left was awkward, but what else were we supposed to do? As angry as I was with Darian, he wasn't wrong. We couldn't force her to reveal her identity and ruin her fantasy evening, even though there's no way in hell we wouldn't have known it was her. Fake tattoos, cut and colored hair, that ridiculous mask... that was still our Car. Her scent and sweet smile alone told me that.

Let's be honest, we never would have accepted an invitation like that if we hadn't known who and what we were meeting up with. Deep down in her soul, doesn't she realize that? For us, it's been her—she's been the only one—since the day she walked into our offices. Yes, we visited a sex club in that time, but we didn't partake of anything offered. It's been a very dry six months for the three of us.

Did she regret our night in the morning light? Was she ashamed about sharing her body with three men? If that's the case, any hope of a relationship between the four of us is doomed. She hasn't returned one of my phone calls, hasn't responded to one of Xander's texts, but Darian promised we will see her at least one more time.

Then yesterday, he informed Xander and I that she's coming to the office at five today to pick up her last check. This will be our chance to give her the safe space she needs to choose us. We've given her more than enough time to think about what she wants—too much time, in my opinion. She has to admit her truth, tell us why she left, and confess our night together. Sure, we could disclose that we know, and knew all along, but then we will never be sure she's choosing us or if she feels backed into a corner.

I can't believe we were her walk on the wild side and nothing more.

I refuse to believe it.

Dear God, please let her choose us.

ENTES TUERE
PUNIRE IMPIOS

Chapter Twelve

CARLISLE

MY HEART PLOPS into my belly as the elevator ascends to the ninth floor. I don't think I'll survive seeing my three men again, but I need my last paycheck and Darian is holding it hostage.

They've called and texted several times since the Monday morning after our night together, but I haven't been able to bring myself to respond.

Hearing Garrett's voice on the recording brought me to tears and forced me back into bed for most of the day.

Xander's text messages simply said, "I don't understand," and sent me to the freezer for a pint of ice cream.

But it has been Darian's radio silence that hurts the most.

Then yesterday, he called and texted—both of the messages he left for me identical, as if he were reading them off a script. "If you want your last paycheck, you will be here tomorrow at five o'clock."

His message brokered no argument, and I knew

better than to try. I responded simply with "Yes, Sir," and hit send before I could think better of it.

The doors open and Garrett's standing there, his face a mask of indifference. I press my lips together, a sudden urge to cry filling my chest, hot tears pressing at the back of my eyes. His gaze takes me in, traveling over my body with a scrutinizing assessment that leaves me cold. "They're waiting for you in the conference room."

I nod, my gaze hitting the floor because I can't take the coldness in his normally bright blue eyes, and walk past him at a condemned man's gait. Obviously, he's angry—maybe disappointed—and his unspoken castigation splinters my already fragile heart. Taking a deep breath, I push open the conference room door. The overhead lights are low, which gives me a small sense of relief. I might not keep the tears at bay, but with the darkness shadowing the room, maybe they will go unnoticed.

Xander looks up from the table, his hazel eyes sharper than Garrett's, a blaze of anger making them sparkle in the darkness. He presses his lips into a tight line and looks pointedly at the chair across from him, telling me exactly where to sit.

I sit down, noting the rectangular pieces of paper in front of me. Garrett walks into the room and takes the seat next to Xander, both men staring at me with a coldness I've never felt from them. Then I notice Darian is sitting at the head of the table, cloaked in the shadows. He's wearing all black and sitting in a black leather chair, his body rigid and still as death.

He speaks without moving a muscle. "Why did you quit?"

I bite my lip and stare at the checks in front of me. One is my normal two weeks' salary, the other is a severance check that is ten times my normal pay. It would set me up for months or longer, considering I get paid double what a normal executive assistant makes in this town. "It's not you guys. I love my job."

"Then why did you quit?" Xander reiterates Darian's question.

"Especially without notice." There's pain in Garrett's voice that pushes a solitary tear out of my eye.

"I scheduled some interviews and sent you potential replacement resumes. Did you interview them?"

"Don't worry about your replacement and answer the question." Xander's hands are clenched into fists on the table.

Throughout all of this, Darian watches me and says nothing.

Swallowing the lump in my throat, I drop my chin to my chest and lean back in my chair, hoping the shadows in the room will obscure my face. "I've been without family for a long time, so the reunion was a big deal. It was my one chance to feel loved and cherished by a family I've desperately wanted for a long time. And it was... amazing."

I press my lips together and study my hands in my lap, memories of having these men's hands on me heating my skin and bringing a blush to my cheeks. "But when I came home, I realized that a one-time reunion wasn't reality, and the family I'm desperate to have, the people I'm desperate to love, well... they have their own lives to live and making space for me isn't realistic."

No one says a word, so I continue. "This epiphany hurt, but it also made me realize I need to get out of here. Out of this town. Out of my head. Out of the mess I've made here. The only thing tethering me to this place is my job—which, again, I love—so I had to quit."

"You're leaving town?" Xander asks.

I shrug. "I thought I'd travel the country for a while."

"More like running away," Darian grits out, his jaw clenched and muscles flexing.

I glance at him, but he's not looking at me. Instead, his gaze is fixed on the table.

"You want a family?" Garrett says, his face softening for the first time. "Why not us? Aren't we a family?"

I can't stop the tears from rolling down my cheeks. "You have been so good to me. I care about you more than you know—"

"And we care about you," his voice softens with every word.

"I think we care about each other in different ways," I shake my head.

Garrett stands up and walks around the table, dropping to his knee beside me. "Don't leave us, Car. We need you."

"If she wants to leave, we have to let her go," Darian says with cold indifference.

I drop my head, fresh tears spilling out of my eyes. I don't know what else I expect him to say, but it hurts all the same. Jenna was right. I never should have started this with a lie, and now I don't know how to get out of the mess I've made. I was so afraid they would reject me if I blatantly came on to them, and none of them have ever come on to me, always keeping it professional in the office.

What a mess I've made of my life.

Xander stands abruptly, which brings my gaze up to watch him as he turns his back to the table.

To me.

"Goddammit," Garrett grumbles and stands up, also walking away from me.

We sit in an uncomfortable silence for a minute or longer before I clear my throat and put my fingers on my paycheck. I slide it off the table and stand, dropping it into my purse. "I guess I'll go."

"Take the severance check, too," Darian says.

"Why? You're not laying me off—I quit. I don't deserve a severance check."

"That's right. You quit on us, not the other way around. Remember that." Darian takes a deep breath and then brings his eyes up to me. "But I don't want to worry about you while you figure out your life. So, take it."

I shake my head, refusing him for maybe the first time, and walk backwards toward the door.

Xander turns around and pins me with a gaze that screams his anguish.

"I can't let it end this way," Garrett says from behind

me, spinning me around and pulling me into his chest. He claims my mouth with all the emotion I feel, and I can't help but melt into him. I moan as he slides his fingers into my hair and drop my purse to bring up my arms, wrapping them around his shoulders. I can't get him close enough. A small cry escapes my lips as he breaks our kiss and brings his mouth to my ear. "Tell us the truth, Car. Tell us how you feel. Please tell us what you want."

My lips part as I look into his eyes. I want to. I want to tell them I'm Ivy, tell them I love them, tell them I want forever. But Darian's words and the conversation I overheard Sunday morning plague me. I shake my head and whisper, "I can't. I'm afraid."

"You can. You have nothing to fear with us. Please, Car. You've already broken my heart once. Don't do it again."

I slide my hand down his chest and rest my palm over his heart. "The last thing I want to do is hurt you."

"Then admit your truth."

"Maybe this will help," Xander says, kneeling beside us over the spilt contents of my purse. At the top is a black and ruby red mask. He fingers the damaged prop that I practically had to tear apart to get off my face, the damned tool of my lies and anonymity, and then lifts his hazel eyes to me.

"Oh god," I gasp, my shoulders slumping as the last of my energy drains away.

Darian stands and takes the mask from Xander's hands. He looks at me for the first time today with the gentleness I know he's capable of. "What should we call you?"

I burst into tears, sobbing in Garrett's firm embrace.

"Don't cry, baby," he coos in my ear.

Darian offers me his hand, which I take, and pulls me into his arms. "Why all the games, Carlisle? Or do you prefer Ivy?"

"You can call me whatever you want—" I sniff against his chest "—as long as you call me yours."

"You are ours. You have been since the day you walked into this office." Xander threads his fingers into my hair and leans forward, pressing a sweet kiss against my lips.

"But we didn't know how you felt, so the last six months have been torture," Garrett says at my back, his lips on my neck.

"I desired you before I even understood what I wanted. I've loved you for a long time."

Darian tilts my chin up and lays his mouth over mine. His kiss is deep and consuming, and takes my breath away. "We love you, too, which is why it hurt so much when you left us."

"I couldn't come back after our night together." I shake my head, casting my eyes on all of them. "I thought I could, but the idea of seeing you after what we shared and pretending like nothing happened was too much for me."

"Do you really think we would have been able to act like nothing happened?" Xander pulls me out of Darian's arms and wraps me up in his embrace. He kisses me softly, his mouth growing firmer and more insistent as I melt against him. Before I know it, he's run his hands down my ass and under my skirt, lifting me into his arms.

I wrap my legs around him without a second thought and scrape my fingernails across his shoulder blades. "I've missed you all so much. This has been the longest three weeks of my life."

"Ours too, sweetheart," Xander murmurs against my skin, trailing kisses down my neck as he sets me on the conference table.

Darian stands at my side and puts his hand over mine, holding it down against the conference room table. "No more running away from us. No more hiding. No more secrets. And definitely no more sex clubs, unless you are with us. Do you understand?"

I nod. "Yes, Sir."

"You're ours, Carli. Forever." Xander kisses me forcefully, pushing me back until I'm lying on the table with my legs wrapped around his hips.

"We're never letting you go," Garrett walks up to the other side of the table, pushing the conference chairs out of his way.

"I'm not letting you go either," I say, glancing between my men, making sure our eyes meet and my intentions are clear.

They are. We exchange knowing smiles that fill my broken heart, making it as strong as ever.

"Do you remember the day you interviewed with us?" Darian says as he flicks open the buttons on my blouse.

I press my lips together and nod, my skin burning with every flick of his fingers.

Xander flashes his wolfish grin and pulls me forward so my pussy presses against the hard cock tenting his slacks. "We wanted to take you that day, right here on this conference room table."

"And now we will, just like we should have so many months ago." Garrett leans forward and kisses my neck, running his lips over my exposed flesh as Darian unfastens the last of my buttons and pushes my blouse open.

"We're going to claim you here once and for all, Carlisle, and after that, we're taking you home and making love to you all night." Darian leans forward and presses his lips to my collarbone.

"Home?"

"Yes. Home with us where you belong," Xander says as he traces his fingers along the edges of my panties before slipping them inside, sliding along my slick pussy. I'm wet and he smiles, a victorious glint in his eyes.

Garrett brings his head up from lavishing my exposed breast. "We have a lot to figure out, Car. Relationships like ours aren't common and most people won't understand, but the simple fact is you belong with us. We want you there when we wake up in the morning and when we go to bed at night—"

"And every minute in between," Darian finishes his thought before claiming my lips.

I moan into Darian's mouth as I ride Xander's hand, a sharp stab of pleasurable pain hitting where Garrett clamps down onto my nipple with his teeth.

Then, I sigh inwardly as my fantasy becomes my reality.

A home and a family.

An unconventional family, but stronger than one I've ever known.

And it's mine.

ENTES TUERE
PUNIRE IMPIOS

DARIAN

We walk through the front door to The Access Club.

In the six months we've been together, living happily as a family, we've been here two times, teasing and testing Carlisle's boundaries with every visit. Of course, we play at home as well, but there's something about this club— call it nostalgia—that seems to take her one step further than she allows herself to go within the confines of our walls.

I walk up to the hostess and give her my card.

She smiles and hands me a room key. "If you're not in a hurry, they're about to start a scene you might find interesting."

I glance over my shoulder at Xander, who is holding Carlisle's hand. Garrett's on the other side, holding her other hand. She's buttoned up tight in a black trench coat, her rich auburn waves pulled up in a demure chignon, a new version of the ruby-red and black mask partially disguising her face.

That's one of my rules—our rules, actually. While we're here, she only takes the mask off in the room. She seems to be fine with this in every way. It provides her with a layer of mental protection and allows her to enjoy herself more fully.

Smiling at Carlisle, I ask, "Do you want to watch a show before we retire to our room?"

She presses her lips together and nods. Watching others gets her hot—needy and desperate for us—so I know Garrett and Xander are good with it, too.

We walk through the heavy curtains and survey the room. I see a table in one of the corner booths and tilt my head towards it.

Xander nods and we walk forward, passing tables without a second glance, until a voice calls out from the darkness.

"Holy shit—Darian?"

I freeze and turn towards the table, shocked to see a guy from our old unit standing up. "Stiles?"

Shaking hands with the lead from Bravo Team 4, my gaze quickly passes over the other two men and a cute brunette nestled between them. I glance over my shoulder as Xander walks up, his eyebrows raised.

"What the hell are you doing in New York?" Xander says, not holding back his suspicion.

I watch as Stiles' eyes travel over my party, a sly grin sliding onto his face. "Xander—" he nods "—G."

His gaze lands on Carlisle and his smile grows wider.

Any other man, any other situation, and I would not like the look on his face, but considering we're sitting in the same sex club with two buddies and a cute little thing they're hovering over, I suppose I'll let it slide.

Besides, they're ex-PsySpecOps like us. It makes sense the three of them are still together accompanied by one special woman.

Stiles tilts his head toward his partners. "You remember Bastion and Romeo?"

"Damn, man. It's been what—six years?" Bastion stands up and shakes my hand while Romeo slides out of the booth, guiding his female companion out behind him.

"More like seven," Garrett smiles and exchanges handshakes, everyone sizing each other up, but not in a territorial pissing sort of way. This is with fresh eyes, as if we are seeing each other for the first time. It shouldn't be a surprise to any of us—it really shouldn't—and yet until this moment, the rumors of the sexual proclivities of our division were just that—rumors.

Now they feel like fact.

Romeo slides his hand onto his female partner's back and guides her forward. "This is Evelyn. Evelyn, we worked with Darian, Xander, and Garrett back in our military days."

She smiles shyly, her eyes quickly glancing over us but locking onto Carlisle. "Hi," she says to no one and everyone at the same time. "I like your mask."

Carlisle touches her face and smiles. "Thanks. I like your outfit."

Evelyn is barely wearing much of anything, but her

outfit is par for the course here at The Access Club. I suppose Stiles, Bastion, and Romeo are cool with the masses feasting on their woman's flesh. That would never fly with Carlisle—I know I couldn't stand it—but to each his own.

Evelyn blushes and dips her head. "Yeah, Bastion and Romeo dressed me tonight."

Bastion flashes a shit-eating grin. "Nobody fucking knows us here—" and then he motions to us "—or at least, we didn't think anybody knew us here. Why not get a little crazy?"

Carlisle reaches out and touches Evelyn's arm reassuringly. "You look beautiful."

The two women share a secret smile.

"Back to my initial question." Xander's voice is gruff. "What are you doing in New York?"

"Yeah, I thought you were down south," Garrett adds.

Romeo shrugs. "We are. We're outside of Nashville running a chain of nightclubs and cowboy bars, but we got invited to the big city by a club owner—this club owner, actually—so we thought we'd make a long weekend of it."

Stiles' gaze never stops traveling between us, as he puts together years of questions in his head. I'm doing the same thing, but with a lot more subtlety. "Do you remember Ken?"

"Ken Walder? Looked like a cross between a GI Joe and a Ken doll?" Garrett laughs.

Stiles nods. "That's the one. He was teamed up with Paddy and LeRoux."

"We remember them. Why?" I ask.

"Well, *they* took over Ken's uncle's ranch in Mountain Love, Tennessee—" Stiles glances at his partners and smiles "—and got themselves a lady named Barbie."

"Shut the fuck up," Garrett snorts.

"Swear to Christ," Stiles holds up two fingers like the scout he once was.

"When are you heading back down south?" Xander asks at about the same time as the submissive walks on stage.

"Monday afternoon."

"Maybe we should grab dinner tomorrow night?"

"We'd like that," Stiles glances at his partners and pulls his phone out of his pocket. "Give me a number and I'll text you."

Garrett gives him his number as the submissive's Dominant takes the stage. Understanding the etiquette surrounding a scene, we nod our goodbyes and take our seats.

I exchange glances with Garrett and Xander, both of whom are as freaked out as I am.

Carlisle reaches over Xander's lap and squeezes my thigh. "Are you okay?" she whispers, glancing between the two of us. "Do you want to go home?"

I put my finger under her chin and tilt her face up, slanting my mouth over hers. She tastes like cinnamon, her favorite flavor and now mine too. "No, pretty girl. We have all kinds of wicked things planned for you in our room."

She grins. "Good, because I've been a very bad girl."

CARLISLE

Darian unlocks our door and precedes us into the room, his head swinging in every direction, his eyes hitting every corner—as I have become accustomed to each of them doing.

My ever vigilant men.

Garrett is on my right side, his fingers interlaced with mine. Xander is on my left, his large hand splayed across my lower back.

Each of my men loves me in their own way.

And wholly, their love is more than one woman deserves.

Garrett is all about physical touch. If we're in a room together, he's touching me in some way. He's the one who holds my hand, throws his arm around me, or wraps me up in his embrace. To the casual observer, most people would think we are in a monogamous relationship, but that's only if they aren't really watching.

Xander is also about physical touch, but he is more possessive and protective. He's usually the one guiding me with his hand on my back, or grasping my hips to move me, or fisting my hair and pulling my head back so I'm at his mercy. He's not much for public display and reserves these touches for home or the office when no clients are around.

Or in a place like this, where nobody bats an eye at our arrangement.

Darian is not physical at all, except for when it's time to be physical. His loving touch comes in a more drive-by fashion when I least expected it. Like when I'm sitting at the breakfast table, he'll walk by and skim his hand over my shoulders, brush my hair out of my face, and give me a gentle kiss on my temple. He rarely claims me in public, unless it's just the two of us, and then he morphs into a rougher version of Garrett, taking my hand and claiming me publicly for all to see.

Each of my men are also very different in how they love me.

Contrary to popular belief, we don't all share a bed every night. Occasionally, I share a bed with Darian, or with Xander, but most nights I fall asleep and wake up with Garrett. It's not because of some pecking order in our relationship. It's because Garrett is a full-on snuggler and likes to hold me close throughout the night. Many times, I'll fall asleep on Xander's chest, but his body temperature runs hot and at some point, I'll roll off of him slick with sweat. Sometimes Darian sits next to me as I fall asleep and sometimes I'll wake up to him stroking my hair, but he rarely sleeps in the bed with us.

It's just not his thing, and I learned early on not to take it personally.

And then there is the way they make love to me. Darian has a quiet dominance to him and speaks with a calm yet authoritative command—inviting no questions, brokering no arguments. He never asks me what I want, instead he tells me what he's going to give me and I fucking love it.

Xander is just as dominant, but in a different way. He'll tell me what he's going to do to me and then, instead of waiting for me to submit, he'll throw me over his shoulder, moving me as he wants, where he wants, whenever he wants. I don't hate it.

Garrett takes pleasure in giving me pleasure. He wants me, however, whenever and wherever possible. There's something unbelievably empowering about knowing that every time somebody looks at you, they're thinking about all the dirty things they want to do with you.

As I said, each man loves me in their own way and wholly, I am loved more than any woman deserves.

"I guess there are more families like ours out there?" I half-state, half-ask after Xander closes the door.

I'm met with silence and turn to see my men exchanging glances.

"Yes." Xander rubs the back of his neck. "But we've never talked about this to anyone other than each other."

"Does our family embarrass you?" Darian unbuttons his suit jacket.

"No, of course not," I mindlessly snap, offended by the insinuation.

He raises his brow and I immediately realize my error. I bite my lip and put my chin to my chest. "No, Sir. I love my family. I love you."

"It would be nice—" Garrett hedges "—to mingle

with people who understand our lifestyle and our family dynamics."

"Why?" Darian grunts, tossing his jacket over the back of the chair as he walks over to the bar. "Why is it anybody's business what goes on inside our home?"

Xander walks up behind me and pulls me against his chest. "We don't give a shit what anyone thinks, but Carli—"

I pull out of his arms. "I don't care—"

"You don't want to care, sweetheart, but you notice the double looks," he pulls me back against him. "I know, because I notice when you tense up."

"But that doesn't mean I care. They can kiss my ass for all I care."

Garrett walks up and slides my mask off my face. "Kissing your ass is our job."

"Everything to do with your ass is our job." Darian winks at me from the bar.

Garrett unties the belt of my trench coat, letting the ends hang at my thighs and then unfastens my buttons, pushing the sides apart. He sucks in his breath when he sees what I'm wearing underneath. "You wore my favorite dress."

I wouldn't call what I'm wearing a dress. At least, it's nothing I would wear in public, as it barely covers my ass —but I knew Garrett would love it. "I wore it for you."

He drops to his knees, running his hands down my thighs and over my calves, removing one stiletto and then the other.

Five inches shorter than I was seconds ago, I tilt my

head back against Xander's chest and smile up at him as Garrett slides his hands up my inner thighs.

Xander wraps his arm around my chest and lays his hand across my throat, lowering his mouth to mine, at the same time as Garrett lifts my leg, hoisting it up on his shoulder, his mouth eagerly moving against my pussy.

I moan into Xander's mouth as Garrett sucks my clit in between his teeth. He knows exactly how to touch me, taking me from mildly aroused to on the verge of coming in less than two minutes.

And I'm always mildly aroused around these three.

In no time, I am writhing, thrusting my hips and riding Garrett's mouth as Xander pins me to his chest, my first of many orgasms tonight crashing over me. Xander releases his hold on my throat and I look down to catch Garrett sitting back on his heels and wiping his mouth, a satisfied smile on his beautiful face.

"Fucking heaven," he gives me a wink.

"I thought we were going to hold off on the orgasms tonight?" Darian comes out from around the bar, handing Xander and Garrett a drink. Then he turns, grabs his own drink and a glass of water for me.

"I couldn't help myself," Garrett says, taking a swig of his Glenlivet.

Xander chuckles at my back as Darian offers me his hand. "Come sit down."

I sit in the wingback chair, my three men crowding around me with their drinks in their hands. "What's going on?"

"It was fortuitous to run into Stiles and his family

tonight of all nights. Don't you think so?" Darian glances to his left and to his right.

Xander nods his head. "Crazy fucking coincidence, but lucky, too."

Garrett waggles his brows at me but says nothing.

"We have something we want to ask you, Carlisle. Something we've been talking about for some time."

I suck in my breath, because this feels like a marriage proposal, but how can that be? Polygamy isn't legal in New York. I'm not sure if it's legal anywhere.

"What's going on?" I ask again, my heart beating hard in my chest, my stomach quivering with tentative excitement and post-orgasm fatigue.

Garrett drops to one knee first, quickly followed by Xander and Darian.

"Oh my god," I gasp.

"We want you to marry us—" Darian starts.

"We want to marry you—" Xander says.

"We don't want you ever to question how committed we are to this relationship," Garrett adds.

"Or to you," Xander finishes.

"Of course, I'll marry you, but I don't need a ring to know you're committed to me."

"Yeah, but—" Garrett takes my hand. "When we put a baby in you—"

"We don't want any problems," Darian finishes for him.

"And we are going to put a baby in you," Xander grins.

"As soon as you're ready," Garrett nods.

I bite my lip, my heart on the verge of bursting. "You want me to have your baby?"

"Babies."

"Oh my god," I bury my face in my hands, tears spilling forth uncontrollably.

"Is that a yes?" Darian chuckles as he wraps his hands around my hips and pulls me off the chair into his lap. Garrett strokes my hair as Xander pulls my hands from my face.

"Yes, to all of it. I want to be your wife and have your babies." I place my hands on Xander's cheeks and kiss him before turning to Darian and then Garrett.

Xander reaches into his pocket. "We got you this."

He flashes a gorgeous platinum ring with three solitaire emerald cut diamonds of equal size. "One diamond from each of us."

Darian holds my left hand out, and Xander slides the ring in place. It's gorgeous, unique, and so very much my men. Xander kisses my hand while Garrett kisses my shoulder and Darian kisses my lips.

I feel infused with a fresh dose of love and acceptance.

Cherished beyond comprehension.

And safe in the arms of my fiancés.

ENTES TUERE
PUNIRE IMPIOS

CARLISLE

"We don't have to hire a new assistant. I can do most of my job from home."

"And when we have clients in the office?" Darian brushes a strand of hair from my cheek and then taps his finger on the tip of my nose.

I narrow my eyes and snap my teeth at his hand. "I'll hire a temp for the next few months and then I can be in the office on the days we have new client interviews."

"The hell you will," Garrett looks up from his seated position, his head laying on the breakfast table, his hand and lips pressed against the cotton t-shirt stretched across my enormous belly.

I glance down at him and give him my *I'm-losing-patience* smile. "Are you saying I can't work and be a mother at the same time?"

"Of course not," he flashes his brilliant blue eyes, a

teasing curve to his lips. "I'm saying there's no reason to do both, and we don't want to stress you out over work when there is going to be more than enough going on here."

"So..." I'm trying to keep the smile from creeping on my face, because what I'm about to say is straight up ridiculous. "You'll be happy keeping me home barefoot and pregnant?"

"Exactly." Garrett ducks out of the way before I can swat the back of his head.

"Sweetheart," Xander takes the now vacant seat next to me and slides his hand between my thighs, disrupting all my thought processes. "What's the real problem here?"

I smile, swallowing down my pride. "That's my desk. My space. You are mine to take care of, and I don't want some tramp coming in, thinking she can take care of you better than me." My voice grows louder with each word despite my best effort to hide the green-eyed monster hiding within my very swollen body.

"Are you jealous?" Garrett's mouth drops open.

"Of someone that doesn't yet exist?" Xander piles on.

Both men laugh, which puts me on the edge of swinging. I clench my fists.

Darian swings my chair around and pins my wrists to the armrests. He leans over me, making me feel small, docile, and completely under his control. "Don't you understand how incredibly lucky we were to find you? To find each other? The odds of three men like us finding our perfect mate are worse than winning the lottery. Do you really think any woman will ever hold a candle to you in our eyes? We know how lucky we are. Do you think we'd ever fuck that up?"

Tears spring to my eyes and damn these freaking hormones.

Garrett's kneeling at my side with his hands on my thigh. "Baby, I'm sorry we laughed, but the idea of you being jealous is ridiculous. Like Darian said, nothing and no one will ever test our feelings for you."

Xander's kneeling on the other side of me and wipes the tears from my cheeks. "No one."

"The only things we will ever love as much as you will be our children." Darian leans forward and kisses the top of my head. "And no hot piece of ass will ever garner a second look. Okay?"

I do this nod-shake thing with my head, which tells no one anything and everything at the same time. "I don't know where this is coming from. I've never been jealous before and I don't doubt you, but the idea of giving up control is making me mental."

"What control are you giving up? Our schedules from nine to five? Who cares? What does that matter when you control us in every other way?" Xander smiles and throws me a wink.

I scoff. "I control you?"

Garrett scoffs back at me. "Fuck yeah, you do."

Darian lets go of my wrists and stands straight, his arms crossed over his wide chest.

"How do I control you?" I motion to the three of them with a sweep of my hand. "Any of you?"

Xander stands up too, his left eyebrow raised high. "Uh, let's count the ways."

Garrett chuckles. "With a bat of your eyes?"

"Purse of your lips," Xander banters.

"Sway of your hips." Darian tilts his head, his eyes tracing over my body, making me hot with that one look.

"The way you trust us," Xander continues.

"The way you submit to us," Darian counters.

"The way you love us," Garrett adds as he also stands up, his hand sliding underneath my hair to cup and massage my neck.

"And last, but not least, the way you take care of us."

"Speaking of taking care of each other," Garrett puts his finger under my chin and swings my face in his direction. "Your breakfast is getting cold."

I glance at the pancakes and then at Garrett's crotch, which is inches from my face. Smiling, I look up at him through my lashes. "I'm not hungry for pancakes."

Xander growls from behind me while Garrett chuckles and shakes his head. "Baby, behave yourself."

I push my lower lip out and pout. "You three have been treating me like a porcelain doll for months. Don't you understand that I'm raging with hormones right now?"

"Oh sweetheart, we know," Xander shakes his head. "We are well aware."

"You'd think three men could keep you satisfied, but your pregnancy hormones are giving us a run for our money." Darian grins and offers me his hands.

I slip my hands into his, letting him pull me to my

feet. He steps into me, his washboard abs hard against my belly. "Do you want us to run you a bath?"

I grit my teeth and push him back, or at least I try to, but he will not be moved. "No, I don't want you to run me a bath."

I swing my gaze to Xander. "No, I don't want a massage."

Then I swing my eyes to Garrett. "And I don't want fucking pancakes."

I clench my hands, tears springing to my eyes again. "I want you to fuck me like you did before we found out I was pregnant! Do you realize how long it's been since the four of us have been together?"

My men exchange glances, but say nothing, which infuriates me even more. I push against Darian's chest again, and this time he takes a step back, letting me storm out of the breakfast nook. I take the stairs as fast as I can, which is still too slow, and storm into our bedroom, slamming the door shut behind me.

Damn these freaking hormones. I don't even know why I'm so angry.

I mean, I know why I'm upset. Ever since we found out I'm pregnant, my men have been different, handling me with kid gloves. The three of them haven't taken me together since I entered my second-trimester. That was five months ago!

Double penetration? Yeah, that's a no go.

Spankings? Nope. Not if you don't count the occasional smack to my ass.

And exploring my boundaries is a thing of the past.

I guess I'm scared that this is it. This is our future.

We went from this amazing, caring, passionate, slightly kinky, albeit unconventional family, to shopping for minivans. Don't get me wrong. I'm thrilled to be having their child, and I know they will be the best fathers ever. Our children will never want for anything and will be raised with more love and attention than most.

But...

For the last five months, I've been having three separate relationships with men who know about each other, accept each other, take care of me together, but we're not *together* together. What if this is the way they see our lives for the next twenty, thirty, fifty years?

Garrett walks into the bedroom first, but Xander and Darian are hot on his tail. They're calm, but watchful, as if they weren't sure what they would walk into and were prepared for anything.

Garrett grabs my hand and leads me to the bed, making me sit beside him on the edge. He interlaces his fingers with mine and brings my hand up to his mouth, kissing each fingertip with that sweet, possessive caress of his. "Baby, we are very aware of how long it has been. Trust me, it's killing us as much as it is killing you, but we don't want to do anything to cause you or the baby distress."

Xander drops to his knees in front of us and runs his big hands up my thighs while Darian takes a seat on the other side of me, placing his hand on the back of my neck, his fingers playing with my hair. He turns my head to him and kisses my forehead. "We have a present for you."

He hands me a beautiful, heavy, black linen envelope with silver and gold embossed edges. Garrett lets go of my hand, and I run my fingers over my name in silver calligraphy. I flip the envelope over to find a red, silver, and gold wax seal holding the envelope closed.

"What is this?"

"Open it." Garrett nuzzles my neck, his breath caressing my skin and sending chills down my spine.

I break the seal and slide out an invitation on red cardstock. In black lettering it says:

You are invited to be ravished by three men,
your men, your husbands, as soon as
possible.
If you accept this invitation, we will attend
to your every need, your every desire and
every perverse fantasy.
There is only one rule:
Be patient with us.
There is no need to RSVP.
Say the word and we are yours,
Always and Forever

Tears stream down my face—damn hormones—but at least this time they are happy tears.

"None of us knew what to expect when you entered

your second trimester." Darian leans forward and kisses the top of my breast where my shirt has fallen open. "Maybe we overreacted, but it's only because we love you so damn much and don't want to hurt you or our child. I promise next time we will be adventurous until you tell us it's time to slow down."

"You still want me like that?" I bite my lip and look up at him.

Xander groans and lays his face in my lap. "Fuck woman. You have no idea the things we want to do to you."

"As soon as it's safe, baby, we will not be gentle," Garrett shakes his head, his lips brushing the side of my neck. Then he sinks his teeth into my shoulder, as if to prove his point.

My cry morphs into a moan as he releases me.

Xander chuckles, his breath vibrating against the apex of my thighs. Then he, too, bites down, not as hard as Garrett, but enough to let me know he feels the same way.

Darian tightens his grip on my hair and claims my lips in a punishing kiss. They have not kissed me like this in months and I miss it so damn much.

"I miss you sometimes," I whisper, but they hear me all the same.

"We are right here, but we get it. Sometimes, I miss you too, sweetheart," Xander says.

"Our lives have to change, because it isn't just us anymore, but that only means we have to be intentional in how we care for you. Be patient with us, have our baby and we'll have you tied up and swinging from a bolt hook in the ceiling in no time," Darian lays his dark eyes on me, his need and desire clear in the dark depths of his gaze.

I smile. "I liked that the last time we did it."

"I know."

"So, about the bath?" Garrett says as he nibbles on my earlobe.

I rub my hand over my belly. Our son decides now would be an excellent time to go for a jog. "Okay. A bath with Garrett first and then a massage from Xander second. What do you want to do, Darian?"

He grins and then licks his lips, his gaze purposely dropping to my lap. "I was thinking I could feed you while you feed me."

And it's at that moment that I remember how damn lucky I am.

Yes, things have been different and will continue to be different as we grow our family. But our love is unyielding and with a bit of patience, I'll still get everything my heart desires.

Foremost, my heart desires my men.

PSYSPECOPS
INNOCENTES TUERE
PUNIRE IMPIOS

The Men of PsySpecOps

PsySpecOps soldiers aren't like other soldiers.
They aren't even like other special ops units.
They're a cross of special ops, Intel, EXO, Cyber, and
psychological warfare, to name a few.

Imagine if Chuck Norris, MacGyver, and B.F. Skinner
all jerked off into a test tube and then impregnated
Wonder Woman.
That's would be them.

PsySpecOps doesn't take volunteers. They recruit the
best of the best out of the special forces units.

They are chosen not only for their physical prowess—
marksmanship, hand-to-hand, endurance, strength,
intelligence, instinct, and ingenuity—but also for their
psych profile that says they'll work best as a team.

They're the Army's answer to a super soldier without chemical injections and gamma rays.

Together, the three men psychologically profiled to be a team are a near perfect soldier—accentuating each other's strengths and eliminating any weaknesses.

Rumor has it, ex-PsySpecOps teams prefer to find and share one woman versus date independently. It is said to be an unexpected side-effect of their training.

They functional perfectly as one in all other aspects of their life, so why wouldn't they want to offer the perfect woman a complete package?

The Men of PsySpecOps work hard, play hard, and love hard... all they need is to meet the special woman who can handle all they have to give.

IS THAT YOU?

Men of PsySpecOps
OUR BRATTY
Queen
Kameron Claire
USA TODAY BESTSELLING AUTHOR

Our Bratty Queen

I'm the bad twin, the loud one, the one dancing on the tables while my critics condemn me. My family rarely knows where I am, much less what kind of trouble I'm starting, which has left me a lonely shell that I fill with my antics.

My sister is my polar opposite in every way. Quiet and in the shadows, she has everyone convinced she's the good twin, but I know better.

When she is kidnapped, my father hires a security team—three hot guys who don't find my antics cute in slightest—and suddenly, I want to the good twin.

I want THEIR attention.

I want THEIR discipline.

I want to be under THEIR control.

We were hired by a billionaire to secure and protect his twenty-two year old daughter who is the identical twin of a high-profile kidnapping. As it turns out, our charge—the social media influencer herself—was the intended victim. Now, we're a hundred of miles away in a secluded cabin that is off the grid, which means our princess has no access to her phone, the internet, or her legion of social media followers. She's bored, she's bratty, and she's begging to be put over our knees and spanked.

She's also everything our domineering hearts crave—the one woman who speaks to our primal need to tame her into the perfect little submissive. If this security detail only lasted a few hours, we could ignore her antics and control our needs—but as the hours spread into days, and she ups the ante to include endangering herself, we can no longer avoid what is in front of us.

This brat needs to be tamed.

She's ours to punish, ours to tame, ours to claim as our own.

KAMERON CLAIRE

USA TODAY BESTSELLING AUTHOR

Our Wallflower Queen

I'm the good twin, the quiet one, the one who hides in the shadows. I never draw attention to myself, never cause my family concern, and most people forget I exist. My sister is my polar opposite in every way. Loud and in the spotlight, she likes to let people believe she's the bad twin, but I know better.

So when I'm mistaken for her, kidnapped and thrust into the spotlight, my three gorgeous rescuers, now bodyguards, are my only protection from the attention I've avoided my entire life—and suddenly, I want to be the bad twin.

I want THEIR attention.

I want THEIR affirmation.

I want THEIR praise.

We were hired to rescue and protect the twenty-two year old kidnapped daughter of a billionaire, but none of us expected to fall in love.

She's everything we've been looking for and more, but we're on the job with a timid and traumatized client, and the number one rule as a bodyguard is *Don't lust after the Client*. Although left unstated, we're pretty sure rule number two is *Don't f^ck the Client*. But the more time we spend together, holed up in a rancher smack dab in suburbia, the harder it is to ignore our feelings, especially as she becomes more dependent upon us, seeking the comfort and physical touch she never received growing up.

She has to know what she's doing to us. She wants our attention, and she's got it. But it's more than that. Our good girl has been lonely her whole life—a quelled bird trapped in a gilded cage with no one to take care of her. We are the men to change that.

And as soon as the threat on her life is dealt with, that's what we aim to do.

She's ours to protect, our to cherish, ours to adore.

Men of PsySpecOps

OUR
SCRAPPY
Queen

Kameron Claire
USA TODAY BESTSELLING AUTHOR

Our Scrappy Queen

I've been stalked by a guy for months who doesn't under the words: Not Interested. But once he escalates his threat by putting my coworker in the hospital, I decide to go on the offensive and give the creep a taste of his own medicine. As a self-proclaimed control freak, I refuse to live in fear and wait for him to come after me. When I sabotage his wooded torture shack, I accidentally blow up the house and the three-month long investigation belonging to the team that's been watching him instead. Of course, I don't know they aren't his goons when we meet, so our introduction consists of me running, cursing, kicking, and punching, only to ultimately lose the fight, but not before I give one a black eye.

We've been tracking this scumbag for three months, waiting for him to lead us to the big fish—the head of the DiFallo human trafficking empire. But when a hellcat blows up our plans, literally, we scoop her up for questioning. She fights us like no woman ever has before, which unfortunately for everyone involved, only turns us on. Her curves are inviting, her tongue is wicked sharp, and her right hook is a thing of beauty—which makes us want to keep her mouth busy while we tether her hands high above her head.

But when we realize she's the scumbag's victim and not an arsonist on DiFallo's payroll, our protective instincts roar to life.

She says she's not interested in our help, but her actions say otherwise, and although we recognize her skill, we can't leave her to take care of this on her own. Not when we're already convinced she belongs with us.

With her life on the line, she has to give up control to us to survive. When she does…

She's ours to protect, ours to fight for, ours to love.

Want more **Witty** Tongues, **Wicked** Needs, & **Wild** Deeds?

Veteran K9 Team

** Military Romance **

Mine to Cherish

Mine to Crave

Mine to Possess

Mine to Adore

Mine to Covet

Mine to Worship

Mine to Protect

Mine to Treasure

Hot Nights with the Boss

** Forbidden Office / Age-Gap Romances **

Dating the Boss

Flirting with the Boss

Teasing the Boss

Tempting the Boss

Rangers Football

Sports Romance

Play Action Fake

Quarterback Sneak

Personal Foul

Two-Point Conversion

Red Zone

Man to Man Coverage

The Men of PsySpecOps

Reverse Harem Romance

Our Bratty Queen

Our Wallflower Queen

Our Scrappy Queen

Our Incognito Queen

Our Enduring Queen (pre-order)

Our Indelible Queen (pre-order)

Our Broken Queen (pre-order)

Our Ageless Queen (pre-order)

Hollywood Lights (Pre-Order)

Billionaire Romance

Show Time (Securing Selyne)

Money Shot

Three Shot

Martini Shot

Long Shot

Grayson Enterprises Series

Bedding the Boss

Enticing the Ex

Tempting the Teacher

Wedding the Widow

Short Story Collections and Bundles

Animal Attraction 4-Story Collection

Vegas Nights 4-Story Collection

Last Stand Saloon 4-Story Collection

Instalove Bundle

Fated Mates of SpecOps Sierra

Paranormal Romance

Riding with the Kodiak

Wild Wolf

Cocky Cougar

Broken Bear

Wanted Wolf

Cursed Cougar

Banished Bear

Fated Mates of Fortune Falls

Paranormal Romance

The Bear's Wandering Mate

The Bear's Fearless Mate

The Bear's Exquisite Mate

The Bear's Resilient Mate

USA Today Bestselling Author Kameron Claire writes stories with witty tongues, wicked needs, and wild deeds. Her paranormal and contemporary books emphasize strong female leads and the protective alpha males who know how to love and support kick-ass, take-charge women. Many of her books contain military veterans, boss babes, dominant men, and goofy K9 hijinks.

Find her everywhere via linktr.ee/kameronclaire
Signed Paperbacks and discounted eBook bundles are available exclusively on her store
Subscribe to the Witty, Wicked & Wild community and read all her books online for as little as $10 a month.

amazon.com/author/kameronclaire

goodreads.com/kameronclaire

bookbub.com/authors/kameron-claire

facebook.com/kameronclaireauthor

instagram.com/kameronclaire

tiktok.com/@kameronclaireauthor